THE FOURTH PRAYER

S. P. Muir

Cover Photo by Ben Hershey @ unsplash

S. P. Muir
Visit my website at www.spmuir.com

ISBN-13 9798565340990

*Dedicated to all those poor souls who are
separated from Christ by their situations
and experiences − or by those who deceive
and mislead.*

"And how will anyone go and tell them without being sent?"

Foreword

Fictional characters are a strange kind of creature. Occasionally, they are based on a real person, but even when a complete invention, their personalities are inevitably an amalgam of people the author has known or encountered. The same goes for locations and events. It is the author's task to weave together real life and imagination, firing the reader's thoughts, and leading them along the story's journey as a willing and enthralled travel companion. In this I can only pray that I've succeeded with The Fourth Prayer.

The main characters in this novel – the four men whose prayers are answered – are not representative of any one person in particular but are indeed amalgams of many. And so, to all intents and purposes, although entirely fictional they are at the same time very real. The same can be said for Catherine Wilmington-Smythe. She is both nobody and somebody. But if anyone were to say, "That's me!" they would be very much mistaken. The same could also be said for the events; they are both fictional and real. And no matter how far-fetched some of them may seem, all of them have happened to somebody, somewhere, and in some way. Many may dismiss Reverend Winters' intense epiphany as nothing more than artistic hyperbole, but I know for a fact that it's not, and so will many others. Many more readers may find the form of domestic abuse I describe to be unreal, and even offensive. They can be reassured, however, that I know of at least three people who have experienced very similar incidents, and have heard from many, many others besides.

The town of Rewford is pretty much in the same vein. It is a fictional place, but apart from its very serious problem, it is representative of several wealthy English market towns – although I have taken quite a few liberties for the benefit of both the plot and its message.

The latter is the most important part of the book – which I felt moved by the Holy Spirit to write. It is a cautionary tale about what *could* happen when our prayers are answered. But ultimately, it is a story about redemption and hope.

Most sincere Christians do not just believe that God answers our prayers, they *know* that he does, albeit in his own good time. Only the Lord knows the right moment to act. Inevitably though, sometimes the answer to that prayer is a resounding *NO*! What if the thing we've asked for could damage us or even go against his will, why would he grant our request? What loving father would give his precious child something dangerous? (Matt 7:11) But what happens if what we *are* given not only benefits us, but is also part of his plan and we reject that gift? What if we've been in the most desperate situation and have prayed for deliverance? If he then provides the path to escape that situation and we allow ourselves to be distracted or led astray, can we then honestly claim that he didn't answer our prayer? Perhaps the four men's prayers in this story can provide food for thought.

May God bless you in the name of our Lord Jesus Christ. Amen.

CHAPTER ONE – *"THOUGH THE POOR PLEAD WITH THEM, THEIR FRIENDS ARE GONE."* *(PROVERBS 19:7)*

John – The First Prayer

"And just who do you think you are, some kind of holy saint?" a small voice sneered in his ear.

Reverend John Harvey Winters just grinned and clattered the dishes all the louder. For some odd reason he liked doing the washing up. He often joked that he wasn't just washing the dishes, he was baptising them. And never had he felt such joy in the task as on this particular evening. Today was a happy day, a special day. It was a day to celebrate. Besides, it was the Sabbath, and not only that, his sermon had gone very well that morning. Yes, it was very much a day to be joyful.

He sensed that the voice was going to speak again so he began singing his favourite hymn in order to drown it out. He had a good voice and the acoustics in their large, modern kitchen always served to compliment it. Somehow the hymn, *How Great Thou Art* always managed to stir his soul. On occasion, the third verse even brought him to tears. This time however, he belted it out with joyous gusto.

"Oh lord my God, When I in awesome wonder,
"Consider all the works thy hands have made..."

Of course, it wasn't a real voice in his ear. It was merely his own subconscious mind expressing the doubts that skulked sulkily beneath the surface of his faith. He knew that he would never banish those qualms altogether, but they no longer had any hold on him. Now, whenever they tried to rise up and undermine his faith, he simply laughed them off. And today of all days, they had no power over him. A little over a year ago, he'd been reborn, and today was the anniversary of the fruit of that rebirth; and he would soon be off to take his turn serving at the soup kitchen he'd started on this very day a year ago.

He was an ordinary looking man; forty-five years of age, of average height and average build with nothing remarkable about his face to set him apart from the crowd. Except maybe for his eyes. They were a soft brown in colour and were wide set which gave his features an honest, friendly appearance. There was a compassion in them that had always been there, but for the past year it had grown so powerful, it seemed to radiate from them and enfold the lost souls he served at the kitchen, holding them in a warm embrace.

"You're going to break them in a minute," his wife, Anne scolded from the doorway behind him. His reply was to sing all the louder. "Oh for goodness sake John," she said, shouting to be heard above the refrain echoing around the kitchen. "Be careful!"

He stopped and turned around to face her, his brown eyes beaming with suppressed laughter. "I am being careful," he chuckled. "Enthusiastically careful."

Anne shook her head in mock despair. "Honestly, John; I wish you'd use the dishwasher. I swear you're a lost cause." In spite of her words she couldn't help grinning.

"And that's why you love me; you never could resist taking in an injured animal."

"I'll injure you all right if you chip my best china."

"Have mercy," John cried, holding up his dripping, rubber gloved hands in surrender. "Think of all the poor destitute souls who'll go hungry tonight if you cripple me."

"I'm sure they'd prefer you not to go. Jenny's much better at it than you – and prettier to boot!"

"Ah, but not as pretty as you, my treasure."

It was almost true, but although Anne was the same age as John, time had definitely taken its toll. Standing just five feet two inches tall, she still had the same petite figure she'd had when they'd married twenty years ago, but her lovely features were now prematurely marred by wrinkles, and her gloriously thick, natural blonde hair had turned grey. And since she stubbornly refused to dye it, it only added to the impression of advanced years. But despite all that, she was still pretty, and nothing could diminish the sparkle in her lovely blue eyes.

"Crawler," Anne replied, giving him a reproving look. "But keep on crawling; I like it." She crossed the room and put her arms around his waist. "I suppose I should let you live," she said smiling up into his face. "I don't like to think of Jenny all alone with those tramps."

It was John's turn to scold. "Now, now, darling; we don't call them tramps anymore. They are the homeless rough sleepers; and there but for the grace of our Lord, goes anyone of us."

Anne sighed. "I suppose you're right. Make sure you wrap up well tonight," she added seriously. "I know it's not that cold but there's a nasty wind blowing all the same. I don't see why you can't use the church hall; at least everyone would stay warm."

"I know, I know. All I can do is keep pestering the bishop. Eventually he's bound to see sense and allow it. In the meantime, we'll just have to make do with the van and the tent."

Anne pushed herself angrily away. "Tent!" she exclaimed bitterly. "That's not a tent, it's nothing more than a glorified windbreak!"

"Be that as it may," John replied consolingly. "It's better than nothing and greatly appreciated by our customers. And we have seats so they don't have to stand around while they eat."

"That was the least old Stuffy could do," Anne sniffed disparagingly.

John shook his head. "I do wish you wouldn't call him that. He's the Right Reverend Richard Anderson; and I just know that one day I'm going to slip up and call him Stuffy to his face."

Anne burst out laughing. "Good! It might just bring him down to Earth."

"Or have us thrown out of our home and queuing up at our own soup kitchen!"

"He wouldn't dare. Now go on, be off with you; I'll finish the dishes while we've still got some left."

"If you insist," John replied meekly. "If I'm going to be sacked, we can't afford to replace them." He peeled off the gloves and handed them to her. As she started to pull them on, he gently lifted her chin and kissed her forehead. "I don't deserve you," he said tenderly.

"And don't you forget it," she replied with a twinkle in her eye.

* * *

The soup kitchen was on the other side of town, but since Rewford wasn't that large a place, it didn't take John more than ten minutes-or-so to arrive. As he pulled into the market square, he could see that Jenny and her helpers – a handful of strapping lads from the local scout troop – were just finishing off setting up. The generator-powered lights illuminated the tent, which as Anne had remarked, was little more than a covered windbreak. A small collapsible table was inside and they were just in the process of putting a dozen-or-so stools around or near it. He slotted his Vauxhall Corsa into a nearby parking space and switched off the engine. He then paused for a few moments to bow his head in prayer.

Despite Anne's justified comments about Stuffy Anderson's parsimonious attitude, John knew just how much he'd been blessed with this mission. It had been remarkably easy to get permission from the local council to use the market square. A couple of phone calls, one letter, and one form to sign. Easy. And then the catering van had literally fallen into his lap. It had been willed to Saint Andrew's church by a much-missed member of the congregation. And the fact that the van had been bequeathed a full month before his epiphany, made John all the more certain that God's hand was at work. Especially as, by a slip of the lawyer's pen, ownership had been passed straight to John himself.

At last he climbed out of the car and strolled over to the kitchen. He zipped his blue parka up as he went, for as Anne had warned, there was a fairly stiff breeze whipping across the square. Jenny saw him coming and gave a little wave. He smiled and raised his hand in return.

"You're late," she said jovially when he reached her.

"Fashionably late, I'd say. And anyway, I'm right on time. I'm not only here before any customers have arrived, I've also managed to avoid doing any heavy lifting. Perfect timing if you ask me."

"Oh, you're incorrigible!" declared Jenny, slapping him on the arm. Her face, red-cheeked from the wind and the exertion, beamed at him all the same. Anne was right to say that she was pretty. She was in her late twenties but looked not long out of her teens. Tall and slender in build, she had long, lush chestnut hair that seemed to cascade out from beneath her green and grey knitted hat. Her large brown eyes were so dark, they looked almost black in some lights.

"I may be incorrigible and I may be late, but I'm here now; so what do you want me to do?"

Jenny looked around. "We're pretty much ready, to be honest. And anyway, you're in charge, so it's up to you what you do."

"Ah, but I was simply being polite and giving you the choice."

Jenny shrugged. "I don't mind."

"Very well then, since it's so breezy, you can stay in the van and cook while I do the serving and clearing away."

"Why thank you kind sir. But don't worry, I'll keep you supplied with cups of tea to keep you warm."

"I should hope so; I think I'll need them tonight." He glanced up at the sky. "At least it shouldn't rain. Have we got some blankets to wrap our customers in?"

Jenny looked a little sheepish. "Yes – at least some. I don't think we'll have enough though. I could only get about half-a-dozen, which is probably half what we'll need. I think we're going to be busy tonight."

"Hmm..." John murmured as he stroked his chin thoughtfully. "I'll see if I can get Anne to rustle up some more." He nodded towards the far side of the square. "And I'd better hurry up," he added as he pulled his phone out of his pocket. "It looks as though our customers are starting to arrive early."

Jenny looked around and sure enough, three indistinct figures were walking through the gloom of the square towards them. "Right then," she said brightly. "I'd better get on."

"And I'll give Anne a call right now. I think you're right; we're going to need all the blankets we can get.

CHAPTER TWO – *"HERE I AM, SEND ME." (ISAIAH 6:8)*

John – The First Prayer

It was exactly one year, six weeks, and two days before his mission anniversary, and Reverend John Harvey Winters was standing in front of the church's large noticeboard. He stood back and scrutinised his handiwork. Yes, he'd done a good job. Not a wrinkle or a bubble marred the notice he'd pasted onto the board. Now he just needed to replace the glass front that kept the weather out; for after all, although they were enjoying something of an Indian summer, it was now September. Once that task was accomplished, he stood back and once again admired the board. Somehow though, he saw *only* the board. He saw how clean the glass was and how neatly the text was printed. The message however, completely escaped his attention. Strange considering he was the one who'd chosen it.

"Come to me, all you who are weary and burdened, and I will give you rest." (Matthew 11:28)

Exactly why he'd picked that particular text was a mystery. After all, it had nothing to do with the series of sermons he was planning to give that month. He'd been sitting at his desktop, casually flicking through Bible Hub, the online Bible site (an excellent resource for all Christians) when it had caught his eye. Of course, it was a well cited scripture, not quite John 3:16 but a good one nonetheless. He'd scribbled a quick note to himself and had then gone back to the tedious task of collating the church finances. Eventually, he'd turned off the computer and had made his way out of the office – grabbing the scribbled note as he left.

And now, three days later, here was the result. And very nice it looked too. As he turned away and began walking along the short path to the gate, the little voice of his doubts whispered in his ear. "It's a nice little career you've got, but face facts, it is really only a job."

He gritted his teeth. "Get thee behind me Satan," he growled quietly. But what the voice had said wasn't that far from the truth. His ministry was becoming – *had* become – little more than a job to him. He did the work; he kept the church, he took the services, he baptised, he married, and he buried. But what had become of his faith? Had it shrivelled under the weight of his responsibilities, or had it never truly been there in the first place? He suddenly stopped dead in his tracks and the true enormity of his doubts crashed over him like a wave. In that moment he realised exactly how much of a charlatan he was. He was a hypocrite. Just like the scribes and the Pharisees in Jesus' day, he was going through the motions without really understanding his role – and everyone knows how roundly our Lord condemned those men!

"No!" he said firmly. "I'm not like them. They hated Christ, but I love him!"

"If you say so."

He swallowed hard, then turned to look at his church. That always helped. It was a beautiful little church with a sizeable congregation. It had the look of one of those ancient Norman buildings, but had in fact been built in the nineteenth century. It was set just a few yards back from a busy street – an oasis of calm amid the chaos of modern life – with a small patch of grass that seemed to serve as a barrier against the passing traffic. And it was *his* church.

Only he – the Reverend John Harvey Winters – had the responsibility for its upkeep and its congregation. He took a few breaths and waited for the calm and the certainty to return. He waited in vain.

Then the awful, terrible truth dawned on him, and it hit him so hard, it knocked him to his knees. Within moments, desperate sobs began to wrack his body and an unstoppable flood of tears cascaded down his cheeks. And then an invisible hand seemed to push him forward as though trying to crush his face into the stone slabs of the path. Several people glanced his way as they walked past the church, agog at the spectacle of the weeping pastor performing some strange rite. He looked more like a Muslim at prayer than a Christian priest.

It seemed to John that this torment went on for an eternity. He ached for it to end but the worst was yet to come. For then all his shortcomings were laid out before him. Yes, in truth he was a good man, but that was not enough. He was a leader and a teacher; and as Jesus' brother James had said:

"*Not many of you should become teachers, my brothers, because you know that we who teach will be judged more strictly.*" (James 3:1)

He knew he had fallen far short of what God expected of him. His despair and anguish became unbearable, worse than anything he could have possibly imagined.

Then he saw – no, 'saw' was too strong a word; he *felt* a face looking down at him, and he instinctively knew whose face it was; and he dared not look into it. How could he? He was guilty; his hands were dirty; his soul was mired in the filth of his sin. And his most heinous crime? Despite his good works and his compassion for his flock, he'd emptied out his faith and replaced it with hubris.

He closed his streaming eyes tight and tried to hide. He prayed. He prayed a prayer such as he'd never prayed in his entire life. He prayed that the torment would end but it was no use, eventually he had to look. And when he did, when he lifted his head and looked into the face that he sensed, nothing could have prepared him for the shock of what he saw without seeing. He was peering into the face of his Lord and Saviour, and that face was smiling at him. Christ's eyes were full of love and grace. It was as though God himself was holding out his hand, inviting John to join him, and offering this wayward pastor the gift of redemption. It was at that moment John realised that in spite of his calling, he'd never truly given himself to Jesus.

But now he could, and now he did. Whole souled and with every ounce of his being he dedicated himself to the Christ. And the wave of relief that swept through him was beyond description. Still he wept, but the tears were tears of joy. He offered himself, such as he was, and in his prayer, he begged to be shown how to do God's will. He echoed the words the prophet Isaiah had written more than two-and-a-half thousand years ago. "Here I am Lord, I'm yours; send me to do your work." And then lifted by the elation, his mission came to him. Everything he needed to do was there in his mind, clearly laid out like a map or a list of instructions. Breathing heavily, he wiped away his eyes and climbed shakily to his feet. He looked around him and was surprised to see that everything looked the same. The lawn and path had not changed, and his church still stood in its faux Norman splendour – no, it was *Christ's* church, not his; for Ephesians 5:23 said that Christ is the head of the church. And anyway, it was just a building; the true church is its members.

At first he was disappointed that the vision – if indeed it could be called a vision – had ended; but then he realised that he could still feel Jesus with him, and when he looked, he could still feel that face smiling at him, and he could still feel the love in those eyes. A wave of emotion swept over him as he fully realised for the first time that that face would never look away; his Lord was with him for all eternity, and would bring him to the Father. The Holy Spirit would dwell within him and would continue to guide his steps, even as it should have done for all these years, had he but allowed it to.

His excitement was uncontainable as he rushed home to tell his wife.

* * *

"Anne, Anne!" John shouted as he burst through the back door into the kitchen. He ran into the long hallway and repeated the cry, not waiting for a reply before he began to mount the stairs two at a time. He was only halfway up when Anne came hurrying out of the lounge door near the foot of the staircase.

"What is it?" she asked anxiously, her eyes wide. "What on Earth's happened?"

"John pulled up short and threw himself recklessly back down the stairs. He rushed towards her, swept her up in his arms and swung her around.

"John!" she snapped. "Will you please tell me what's going on?"

He put her down, held her by the shoulders, and beamed joyously into her puzzled face. "Nothing; everything!"

"John!"

"Anne, I've been such a fool, but now the Lord has opened my eyes."

Anne started to relax. Clearly there had been no disaster; her husband was happily excited about something but he was certainly behaving very oddly. His joy was positively contagious though, and she couldn't help smiling back at him.

"Well I know you're a fool – you've always been a fool – but since you're not Saint Paul, I don't understand what you mean by, 'opened my eyes.' And anyway, you've never even been to Damascus."

"How do you know?" he asked with a chuckle. I might have travelled all over the world before we met."

"We were seventeen when we first met, and you were pleasantly boring even then. Now calm down and tell me what's happened."

So tell her he did. And as the episode poured from his lips, so the tears again began to flow from his eyes. Anne studied his face the whole time, carefully assessing whether he was joking, serious, or just plain mad. Perhaps the strain of work had got too much for him. In the end though, there was no denying the veracity of both his tale and his sanity.

When he finally explained his new mission, she raised a sceptical eyebrow. "A soup kitchen? In Rewford? Darling, this isn't a sprawling city like

London or Manchester. This is a medium sized market town populated by wealthy middle-class pensioners and families. While I appreciate what you want to do, I'm not sure it's needed here."

"Oh, it's needed all right; *he* told me it's needed."

Anne reached up and gently stroked his damp cheek. "Honestly John, have you ever even *seen* a tramp in Rewford?"

"No; not that I can remember. But as the saying goes: 'Build it and they will come.'"

Anne blew out her cheeks and studied his face again. His enormous excitement almost overwhelmed the earnest certainty in his eyes; and she wasn't entirely convinced by his 'vision'. She was a dyed-in-the-wool Anglican, and this sort of thing was far too Happy-Clappy to her way of thinking. But then John had always been of the same mind.

"Very well then," she said at last. "What do we need to do first?"

John's smile grew even broader, and his heart swelled with love for his wife. He couldn't help noticing that she'd said, 'We'.

CHAPTER THREE – *"IF ANYONE WOULD BE FIRST, HE MUST BE LAST OF ALL AND SERVANT OF ALL." (MARK 9:35)*

John – The First Prayer

John watched the three men as they approached the catering van. He recognised them all because they'd been the first regular visitors to the kitchen, and among the few who hadn't eventually moved on. Jerry, Sticks, and Derek, those were their names – at least so they said. John had quickly come to realise that many of his customers now lived by different names to the ones they'd been given. Jerry and Sticks had been the only two customers on that first night, with Derek joining them just two nights later. The former two were now carrying what were obviously their entire belongings with them. Only Derek was empty handed.

Jerry put John in mind of so many of the homeless he'd encountered over the past twelve months. They were former service men, emotionally damaged, traumatised by the things they'd seen and done, and then abandoned by the country they'd served so heroically. Almost all of these tragic wrecks of humanity turned to drink or drugs in an effort to assuage the guilt or ease the pain that plagued their psyche. Of all the men he met – and these ones were always men – they were the ones his heart ached for the most. But although the months had definitely taken their toll on Jerry, physically he'd not deteriorated as much as most, and he'd certainly not turned to alcohol or drugs. He must be mentally stronger than most, and if he *was* an ex-serviceman – and the large, khaki duffle-bag evidenced that he was – perhaps his survival training was helping him to endure.

At most in his mid-to-late teens, Sticks was by far the youngest, and he was also the frailest of the trio. John had watched this young man's condition change over the last twelve months; at first with feelings of pity, then of hope, and now finally with despair. A year ago he'd obviously been fairly new to the streets and had been reasonably healthy, but he'd been quiet and morose, and obviously very fragile. And the poor, frightened boy had quickly crumbled as the reality of his new life had begun to bite. John had tried his best to steer him towards the help he so desperately needed, but it seemed he'd been a lost cause. The boy had been oblivious to John's offers. But then something had changed. Suddenly, he'd begun to look a little brighter, a little healthier. For a few short weeks John had begun to think that there was hope for the boy. But then something had clearly gone very wrong, and from then on, his deterioration had been precipitous. He was now frighteningly thin, and dirty beyond belief. He'd also now developed a pronounced limp. His sole possession appeared to be a filthy sleeping bag that he carried in a tight roll under his arm. His clothes were now crumpled and filthy, and although his parka was the same colour and style as John's, if the reverend hadn't seen it a year ago, he would never have been able to tell. John wasn't sure how much longer Sticks would last. If this unseasonably warm autumn turned into a repeat of the arctic conditions of eighteen months ago, John was certain the boy would not survive. His condition put him in mind of how Derek had been when he'd first seen him.

And there was a puzzle. Derek had seemed close to the end a year ago, yet now he was the fittest of the three. His clothes had seemed little more than filthy rags and he'd been so emaciated, he'd looked as though he'd just escaped from a Nazi concentration camp. But even so, there had been something in his eyes; something that told John he'd not quite given up hope. And soon after he'd arrived, just as with Sticks, he had begun to change. Not a change that was immediately obvious, but a steady and gradual improvement. John would have loved to believe that it was the effect of the soup kitchen, but such hubris was now behind him. Perhaps it was that coat Derek had one day turned up in.

John studied the man standing at the open hatch of the van carefully. He was by far the eldest of the three men; perhaps in his late fifties, but more likely, his early sixties. But it was hard to be sure; life on the streets was incredibly hard and could age someone alarmingly fast. Although John couldn't see it, he knew he had fine and balding, steel-grey hair, but he could see Derek's equally untidy grey beard. He looked as though he'd now put on a good amount of weight, but it was hard to tell beneath the bulk of his coat. And what a coat it was! Light blue in colour, it was luxuriously puffy and looked to be both warm and waterproof. It had a good hood too, with drawstrings that were now pulled tight against the breeze. It was clearly top quality and would have been enormously expensive. Derek had also managed to keep it unusually clean. John had no idea where he had obtained such a wondrous garment, and he didn't want to know. Sometimes it was best not to ask. But for whatever the reason, there was now something more than just a physical change about the man. Derek's demeanour had also been improved. There was now a steady calm in his grey eyes that could almost have been contentment had he not been in such a parlous situation. John yearned to know the secret of Derek's transformation but knew better than to ask. Maybe one day he would tell John the tale on his own volition.

He suddenly realised that he hadn't welcomed his guests. Scolding himself for his bad manners he made his way over to the van.

"Evening gents; looks like it's going to be an unpleasant night."

The response from each of the men was markedly different. Jerry acknowledged him with little more than a casual nod, but Derek turned and spoke.

"Evening Rev," he said with a soft smile. His voice was barely audible above the sound of the wind.

Sticks, however, just looked down at the ground, his emaciated body hunched against the cold. There was a worrying absence in the boy's face, clearly visible in the light shining from within the van. John quickly made a decision.

"Jenny, when you've made the boys here a cuppa, can you pass me out three blankets. They can go and sit out of the wind while you're preparing the food. It's all right lads," he added addressing the three men. "I'll bring your grub over to you when it's ready."

Again, Jerry gave nothing more than a slight nod of thanks, but Derek spoke a few words of gratitude, although John couldn't quite hear what they were. His smile clearly conveyed their meaning, however. Sticks though, continued to stare sightlessly at the ground.

"The blankets are on the passenger seat," Jenny replied. "You can grab them while I get things done here."

"Okay, no problem."

In no time at all, the steaming cups of tea were handed to the men. They sauntered over to the tent with John following them with the blankets. Once they were seated, he passed one to each man. When he came to Derek, he hesitated. It seemed pretty pointless putting a blanket on top of such a marvellously warm coat.

The old vagrant immediately understood his benefactor's uncertainty. "If you don't mind Rev," he said in his curiously calm but thin and cracked voice. "I'd like to lay it around my legs. They get awful chilly these days."

"Of course you can. Have you tried wearing long johns? They might help a bit."

Derek's smile grew much wider revealing badly discoloured teeth. "Already do – and two pairs of trousers. Doesn't seem to help much though."

"I don't suppose it does given the circumstances," John conceded sympathetically.

Jerry let out an obscene profanity then added, "You're a damn sight better off than the rest of us with that bloody coat of yours."

"Please, Jerry," John admonished. "Can you moderate your language a bit; Jenny might have heard you."

"Yeah, if you say so." Jerry's tone made it quite clear that he didn't give a stuff whether Jenny heard him or not. John pretended not to notice.

Here, Rev," Derek said giving John's sleeve a tug. "I was just thinking; I don't suppose you could bear to part with one of the blankets, could you?"

Jerry glared at the old man. "What, you mean your coat isn't warm enough?" he asked incredulously.

"Not for me, Rev," Derek continued, ignoring the jibe. "I'm thinking of the lad here. That sleeping bag of his ain't up to much anymore."

"I'm not sure we can, Derek. We've only got a handful as it is, and I think we'll have need for them all tonight – and more."

"Ah, I see. Shame though, don't you think?"

John studied the unfortunate boy thoughtfully. Perhaps Anne would be able to rustle up enough to have one to spare. "I'll see what we can do."

"There's too damn many of us in Rewford now," said Jerry bitterly. "Once news of you got out, they've come from all over the place. I used to get a fair few quid from passers-by; I'm lucky to get just a dirty look these days. People soon get fed up being pestered for spare change from every other doorway. The poor kid here hasn't got a chance."

John had to admit that Jerry had a point. The number of the homeless and destitute in the town had burgeoned in the course of the year. But then again, despite the drawbacks, that did mean his mission was reaching many more than it otherwise would. And wasn't a guaranteed nutritious hot meal better than a few extra pounds to spend on alcohol or drugs?

A movement from the van caught his eye. Jenny was waving to tell him that the food was ready.

"Ah, grub's up," John said cheerfully. "I'll go and fetch it for you."

"I'll give you a hand," Jerry said in a grudging voice. But John had a strong feeling that his unenthusiastic tone was an affectation, and that Jerry was actually glad to be of help.

As they walked towards the van, John glanced at the man beside him. His gait made John even more convinced that he'd once been in the services – most likely a soldier.

"Poor Sticks is in a bad way, isn't he Jerry?"

Jerry snorted contemptuously, but there was a note of sympathy in his voice. "You'll be wasting a blanket on him, that's for sure. It won't make much difference to him now."

"Perhaps not; but it might make him a little more comfortable. And the longer he can keep going, the better chance he has of a change of fortune."

"I wouldn't hold your breath waiting. I've seen too many like him. He'll be lucky to last a few days if the weather really turns again. A few severe frosts and he'll not make it to Christmas, let alone the spring."

John sighed heavily. "Perhaps you're right; we can only pray that you're wrong."

"Prayer!" Jerry scoffed. "Don't make me laugh, chaplain. No offence, but get down on your knees and you're just talking to yourself."

So there it was; he'd called John, 'chaplain'. So he *had* been in the forces after all. "You don't believe in God then Jerry?"

There was no reply, but by the way the ex-soldier clenched his jaw, John could tell there was a story there to be told; but it was a story he'd probably never hear.

CHAPTER FOUR – *"THE ENEMY SAID, 'I WILL PURSUE...I WILL DRAW MY SWORD; MY HAND SHALL DESTROY THEM.'"* (EXODUS 15:9)

Jerry – The Second Prayer

It was exactly one year and two days before Reverend Winters' mission anniversary, and Jeremy Richard Dawson was standing on the fringes of Frinton Wood waiting for the sun to rise. It had been a clear, starlit night which meant a cold, crisp morning. The brightening skyline indicated that there were just a few short minutes left to wait. And then suddenly, there it was; the bright, dazzling sliver of gold bursting forth and climbing gloriously into the sky. So magnificent was the sight, it almost lifted Jerry's spirits. Almost.

He'd been living in the expansive woods for almost a month now, putting his hard-won survival skills to good use. Over the past few days however, a mounting sense of unease had eventually led him to the decision to move on. That decision had finally been made the previous afternoon. His carefully hoarded provisions had been running low for some time and were now all but exhausted. And he was fairly certain that the heat would have died down by now, which meant it would be safe to make his way into town. So after he'd eaten a meagre and disgusting meal of fried slug and earthworm made slightly more palatable by a garnish of wild sorrel and blackberries, he'd packed his military holdall and settled down for a last night in his carefully built shelter.

It had been a cold and uncomfortable night, full of the horrific nightmares that always haunted his sleep; except strangely, this time he didn't mind; it meant he'd be up and ready to go in time to see the sunrise. It was something that had always filled him with awe; and even now, amid all his troubles, it turned his thoughts to higher things. But within a heartbeat the old bitterness rose up and quashed such idiotic thoughts. He'd seen too much, been through too much, and had done too much to think along those lines. With a fierce and resentful grunt, he shouldered his pack, turned his back to the sun and started off across the muddy field.

His intended destination was the town of Rewford which seemed perfect for his needs. It was big enough to disappear into the background, yet small enough not to have too much in the way of CCTV. It was also a long way from his old life in Kent – and the further away he was from there, the safer he would be.

It was going to take a good many hours to reach Rewford, perhaps even most of the day. But since the weather was so fine, Jerry didn't mind; he was used to long marches. And he'd saved a packet of peanuts and a small bag of dried raisins for the journey. That was a good fifteen hundred calories – certainly enough to keep him going until he got there. But then he'd be arriving with nothing else and no money to buy as much as a sandwich. He cursed himself for the umpteenth time for not making sure his wallet was in his pocket when he'd fled his home. But what was done was done, and there was no point in beating himself up about it.

At first the going was difficult, for although the mud in the field was reasonably dry, it had been roughly ploughed which made each step a little precarious. Even so, within half an hour he reached the lane that led down to the main road just a couple of miles away. From that point, it was only another twelve miles or so to Rewford itself. He smiled to himself. A total of fourteen miles on well-maintained roads was going to be a cinch. Compared to what he'd faced so often in Afghanistan, it would be like a walk in the park.

His face fell as his thoughts returned to his old army days. The faces of the friends he'd lost and the men he'd killed haunted his dreams almost every night. And even when awake a sudden flashback could jump out and ambush him like a Taliban trap. The tours had been long and the R and R always too brief. And every time he'd returned home, his relationship with his wife had become more and more strained. Even civilian life had got progressively worse until...

Leanne had always been difficult to live with, which meant the marriage had been dogged with some form of spousal abuse from the start. At first it had been vocal, but had soon become more physical. Perhaps, he mused as he walked purposefully down the narrow lane, his long spells abroad had been a blessing after all. Even after the UK had finally left Afghanistan there'd been other out of area stints. But then six months ago the time had come for him to leave the army, and then things had gone from bad to worse.

The only job he'd managed to get was agency work. And all they'd given him was a job with a haulier, hosing down their trucks. His frustration had become a dark and deadly creature in its own right, poised ready to explode into life when the time arrived.

The violence that had raised its ugly head as regular as clockwork had been growing in intensity each time, until eventually, just a few short weeks ago, he'd snapped. He'd struck her full force with two hard punches to the head. And they'd been *very* hard punches indeed. She was only small, and the force of those two sledgehammer blows had sent her crashing into the wall with a terrible force. She'd then crumpled to the floor where she'd lain limp and frighteningly still.

For a few seconds he'd gawped at her inert body, horrified at what he'd done. Then in a flash he'd dropped to his knees beside her, checking her carefully for signs of life. To his immense relief she was breathing normally, but from the way he'd hit her, there could well be bleeding inside the skull or swelling of the brain. She needed medical care and fast. He'd pulled out his mobile phone but had suddenly frozen. He knew he'd be in deep trouble over this – he might even end up in prison. His thoughts had raced as he'd looked around the sitting room. His eyes had fallen on the landline phone on the table, and a plan had sprung fully formed into his mind. He'd carefully pulled Leanne's unconscious body over towards the table and had placed her into the recovery positioned. Then as fast as he could, he'd rushed around the house throwing together the things he was going to need for his escape. Only hours later did he realise his wallet was not in his coat pocket where he'd been sure that he'd left it.

Less than five minutes later he was back with Leanne. He'd checked her vital signs again – there'd been no discernible change – then he'd picked up the receiver and had dialled three nines.

"Emergency, which service?"

"Ambulance," he'd breathed softly.

"I'm sorry, was that ambulance?"

"Yes," he'd replied in an even quieter whisper.

"One moment please."

He'd then placed the receiver on the floor beside her, and had bolted for the door. The emergency services would be able to trace the address from the phone number, and an open but silent line would be sure to get priority status. When the ambulance arrived, if she was still unconscious, they might assume that she'd tripped and hit her head as she'd fallen. That, he'd hoped, should give him time to put some distance between himself and his crime.

Now, as his boots beat out their steady rhythm on the lane's road surface, he grimaced resentfully. He visualised the hardened feminists in their various organisations screaming out about domestic violence. There was probably even one called, 'Women Against Ex-Soldiers Who Punch Their Wives'. But what did they know? What did Leanne expect would happen?

For seven years he'd put with it. Every month on the dot she had transformed from a lovely sweet-tempered woman into the girl from 'The Exorcist'. At first, she'd screamed and shouted at him, flinging all kinds of hateful accusations his way. But then had come the first slap. It had caught him completely unawares, leaving an angry red handprint on his cheek. She'd made to follow it up with another but he'd managed to grab her wrists. He'd then spun her around, wrapping his arms around her and holding her tightly and impotently in his embrace. She'd struggled to break free for several minutes, kicking and screaming at him the whole time. Eventually though, she'd stopped struggling and had started to cry. When he'd finally let her go, she'd fled upstairs to their bedroom and had slammed the door shut. And from then on, the episodes had got much worse. Although he'd usually managed to restrain her when she'd flipped out, thrown objects were more of a problem. His fractured wrist came curtesy of an accurately launched, cast-iron skillet.

She'd always apologised, promising it would never happen again, but only when she'd hurt him. And as with most victims of domestic abuse, he'd always blamed his (thankfully few) injuries on his own clumsiness; but one day he knew that the truth was out. His friend, Alan, had taken him aside in a pub. He had told him he'd overheard his own wife, Chrissy, gossiping about it with a group of her friends.

"And you know his broken arm," Chrissy had said, exaggerating the injury. "Leanne said she did that by walloping him with a dirty great frying pan."

"And that's not the worst of it mate," Alan had said with a wry grin. "They were all going, 'Oh poor Leanne, it's such a shame.' And 'Yeah, the poor girl gets such horrible PMS.' They didn't give a monkey's about you mate! In fact, they were all laughing at you."

This final incident though – the last straw – had occurred when he'd had the temerity to enquire as to where she'd put his boots. She'd hurled abuse at him, furious about 'being treated as his skivvy'. She had then stormed out of the room presumably to go and find them.

"You only had to tell me where they were," Jerry had called irritably. "I'd have gone and got them myself."

That had been a bad mistake. She'd then come flying at him, shrieking like a vengeful banshee and had attacked him with the heavy, military boots.

And then he'd hit her.

And now as he walked along in the bright early morning sunshine, he suddenly stopped dead in his tracks. Suddenly the true enormity of what he'd done crashed over him for the first time. And his monstrous hypocrisy was as bad – if not worse – than his crime.

He'd always despised men who hit women or children. He hated any kind of bully, but they were the worst. As far as he was concerned, they were nothing but scum – cockroaches that needed to be exterminated. He'd once tracked down a victimised woman's ex-boyfriend and had beaten him to a pulp. The unfortunate bully was then on notice that if the girl so much as broke a fingernail, a party of vengeful squaddies would descend on him. And neither would they have a problem getting rid of his body. And as far as Jerry knew, that was the end of her problems.

But now he was just as bad. He'd become the one thing he hated most. For all he knew, Leanne had suffered a brain haemorrhage, and was now dead. He wasn't only a wife beater; he was a murderer. He fell to his knees and began to weep bitterly. Somehow, he managed to crawl to the edge of the road where, with the tears still pouring down his cheeks, he vomited violently, spattering the weeds with his guilt.

Eventually, he raised his eyes to the clear blue October sky and for the first time in three years, the one-time Corporal Jeremy Richard Dawson began to pray. But it was a prayer unlike any of those he'd said with the army chaplain. They had been shallow, even mechanical. This one came from the deepest pit of his despairing soul.

"God," he pleaded miserably. "I don't know if you're real or not, but if you are, I need your help. I've really screwed up my life. If you are there God, throw me a lifeline so I can pull myself back on track. Please God, if you help me, I'll do anything you ask."

Whether or not there was a God, and if there was, whether or not God heard him, Jerry was given no sign. After a while though, he pulled himself back together, and climbed shakily to his feet. Then, after a few deep breaths, he continued on his way.

CHAPTER FIVE – *"SO IT WAS...THAT JESUS HIMSELF DREW NEAR... BUT THEIR EYES WERE RESTRAINED, SO THAT THEY DID NOT KNOW HIM."* *(LUKE 24:15, 16)*

Jerry – The Second Prayer

I t was getting dark by the time Jerry reached the outskirts of Rewford. Following the main road towards the centre of town he was relieved to see that the houses were large, well-to-do, and nicely middle class. That augured well for gleaning some change from passers-by. Not that there would be much chance of that tonight. First, he needed to find the town centre, have a good look around and locate a good spot to bed down. From what he'd seen in London, doorways seemed to be the preferred spot. But he was now very tired and extremely hungry. Somehow, he needed to find food. A long, cold night with aching legs and an empty belly held no appeal at all. Still, he'd had worse when he'd done his special forces training in Wales. His face hardened. He'd managed to screw that up as well! He'd been hoping to join the SAS, but in the end he'd failed miserably. Mind you, the skills he'd learned that week had come in handy.

Within the hour, he passed a petrol station and his heart skipped a panicked beat. A grey Ford Focus, identical to Leanne's was just pulling up at a pump. Since it was on the far side of the island, he couldn't make out the number plate, but in the bright lights of the forecourt he could clearly see the woman driving it, and he was positive that it was his wife. The same round face framed by the same dark hair, cut in the same style. It was all he could do to keep walking. Stopping to stare would only have drawn attention to himself. He kept his face straight ahead but his eyes flicked continuously towards the garage.

When the woman finally emerged, he let out a sob of relief. It most definitely was *not* Leanne. This woman was much taller and was somewhat plump.

Once he'd got over the shock, he kicked himself. The chances of Leanne just happening to be in a town a hundred miles from home and pulling into a petrol station at the exact moment he was walking past were so astronomical as to be impossible. And anyway, if it *was* Leanne, it would mean he was off the hook for her murder. He quickly put the thought out of his mind and lengthened his stride. The sooner he hit town, the better.

In fact, it was only twenty minutes later when he arrived at the town centre. Although the shops were now shut or in the process of shutting, there were still plenty of people around. He hadn't gone far before he caught the unmistakable smell of fish and chips. His mouth began to water uncontrollably and his belly rumbled like distant thunder. Drawn towards the enticing, irresistible aroma like a moth to a flame, he soon rounded a corner and there it was. A chip shop. For a few moments he stood staring through the window, transfixed by the sight of all manner of deep-fried delicacies. But which ones would he choose if he had the money? The answer was obvious: *all of them*!

The sound of laughter at his back distracted him from his gluttonous reverie, and he turned to locate its source. It came from a young man and his girlfriend who were sitting on a little seat beside what looked like a bandstand. And oh, the pain and the delight; they each had a portion of chips in their hands and were tucking into them with mucho gusto. He watched enviously for a moment or two before hunger finally got the better of him. He strode across the road and approached the young man.

"Could you spare a chip or two please mate? I wouldn't ask but I haven't eaten for a couple of days now."

"What?" the lad asked with a touch of wary hostility.

"You can have mine," the girl said with a sympathetic smile. "Silly cow covered them in salt and vinegar and it's totally spoilt them."

"Are you sure?" Jerry asked, somewhat taken back by her generosity.

"Yeah, of course," she replied handing over the unwrapped paper and its wondrous contents. "I'll keep my sausage though," she added taking back the huge, batter-covered banger.

The young man was suddenly put to shame. "Here you are mate," he said not to be outdone. "You can have a bit of my fish." Carefully he broke off a small piece of cod and placed it on top of Jerry's chips. "Bon appetite."

"Thank you so much," Jerry gushed, unable to believe his luck.

"You're welcome," the girl said with a beaming smile.

"Good luck," the lad called as jerry walked away. But his words barely registered with Jerry, for he was already lost in a world of culinary bliss. No banquet, not the richest, most expensive delicacy on the planet could ever have tasted as good as that freely given, charitable gift. And he then saw something almost as good – or perhaps even better. It was a small empty shop located in a nice, well-trodden street not far from the station. A perfect spot to beg. He grimaced; how he hated that word! And just to top this sweet little cake off with a nice plump cherry, there was an A4 size poster in the window which read in large letters:

Free soup Kitchen 10 PM Market Square.
Open every night from Saturday 20th October.
Hot food and drink for those in need.

Brilliant. All he needed now was a place to wash and a place to sleep. But then hadn't he passed a little sign saying 'Public Toilets' just a few minutes ago? That would take care of keeping relatively clean, but as for a place to bed down warm and dry...

In a burst of inspiration, the picture of the bandstand flashed into his mind. It was bound to have a space underneath it; and he had a feeling he'd spotted a small breach in the panelling behind where the chip-girl and her boyfriend were sitting. If he could find a way in, that would be ideal. It also occurred to him that he hadn't seen any other down-and-outs in his brief exploration of the town. He drew a deep breath and slowly let it out. What a stroke of luck. Clearly Rewford had been the perfect choice.

But whether or not this bounty of good fortune was God's answer to his prayer would perhaps, always remain a mystery to him. Not once did the thought of the Almighty cross his mind.

CHAPTER SIX – *"SO THE POOR, LIKE WILD DONKEYS, SEARCH FOR FOOD IN THE DRY WILDERNESS." (JOB 24:7)*

Sticks – The Third Prayer

Sticks barely noticed when Jerry placed the steaming paper bowl in front of him. Only when Derek dug his elbow into the stricken, emaciated boy's ribs did he surface from his heroin riddled reverie. He glanced at the old man sitting beside him and then down at the table. Food; hot food. He wondered why he hadn't realised it was there. After all, it was the one thing he'd been looking forward to all day. Apart from scoring his wrap of smack of course – or skag, as his Scottish dealer called it. And not just soup, there was a corned beef sandwich to go with it. His stomach rumbled uncomfortably as he picked up the plastic spoon and began to eat.

Although it was called soup, it was more like a lentil and vegetable stew – and a very tasty stew at that. But as hungry as he was, Sticks found it difficult to force it down. He knew he was sick, but had no idea as to just how ill he really was. He had a hacking cough that only seemed to subside when he smoked smack – chasing the dragon, as it was called. The drug also eased the pain in his foot, but more importantly, it blunted the edge of his mental anguish.

"How did you hurt your leg?" John asked as he sat down opposite him.

Sticks lifted his head and managed to focus on the reverend's gently smiling face.

"Don't know," Sticks replied somewhat croakily. "It just started a few days ago and it's got steadily worse."

Derek at his side gave him a gentle nudge. "Tell you what lad, why don't you take a stroll down to the hospital later. Let A&E take a look at it. You might have an infection or something."

"Yeah, maybe I will."

It was clear from the tone of his voice that he had no intention of going. John watched him for a moment, his heart filled with pity for the poor wretch of a boy. A sudden thought came into his mind.

"I tell you what, hang around until we close up and I'll drive you there."

Sticks studied John's earnest, friendly face for a moment and then shook his head. "No, you're all right; I'll get down there eventually."

John drew a deep breath and bit his lip. He knew the kid had more problems than a sore leg, and was probably too frightened to go without help. He made a sudden decision.

"Right, I'm going to take you now. As soon as you've finished your soup, we'll be off."

Sticks watched in horror as John jumped up and hurried over to the van. He clearly needed to make his escape fast. He dropped his spoon and started to get up but was pulled back down into his seat from either side. Both Jerry and Derek had caught hold of his coat to prevent him leaving.

"It's all right, son," Derek said reassuringly. "It'll be best to let him take you."

"Come on lad," Jerry added gruffly. "Finish your grub."

Reluctantly, Sticks recovered the spoon and began to eat. Slowly and mechanically his hand rose and fell, spooning the thick, nutritious broth between his cracked, scabby lips. It took him some time to finish it, but that was of little consequence since there were now several more customers for John to see to. It also gave Anne time to arrive with a good armful of blankets. Sticks watched on curiously as the discussion between the reverend and his wife progressed. He drew a deep, fearful breath when John gesticulated in his vague direction. Anne then looked at her watch and said something harsh in reply while cocking her head in clear disapproval. Her husband then put his hands on her shoulders in a reassuring manner and kissed her forehead before walking back towards the table.

Sticks scraped up the last spoonful of soup then looked resignedly up at John. He nodded his readiness, and got slowly and painfully to his feet.

"Don't you want your sandwich?" Derek asked casually.

Sticks shook his head. "Can't seem to manage anything else. You can have it."

"You sure?"

Sticks nodded. He then reached down, gathered up his sleeping bag, and limped away with John holding his elbow.

"Good luck boy," Derek called after him.

"Yeah, see you here tomorrow," Jerry added.

Sticks acknowledged them both with nothing more than a flippant wave of his hand. Within moments he was safely ensconced in the passenger seat of John's Corsa.

"Right then," John said brightly as he put the car into gear. "Let's away. The doctors will have your leg sorted in no time."

"My foot," Sticks mumbled as he closed his eyes. "It's my foot that hurts."

"Foot then," John replied with a grin. "They'll have your foot sorted..." He left the sentence hanging in the air. It was clear that the poor boy had immediately fallen into a deep and troubled sleep.

* * *

It took no time at all to reach the hospital, but finding a parking space there took considerably longer, despite it being a quiet Sunday night. John thanked the Lord it wasn't a Saturday. They'd have had no chance of finding a spot then.

"Wakey-wakey," John chimed, giving his sleeping passenger a shake. There was no response. "Sticks, wake up," John repeated giving the boy a firm shove. To his relief, Sticks groaned, opened his eyes and peered myopically around them.

"Oh right," the boy mumbled and then began to fumble unsuccessfully with his seatbelt.

"It's all right; it gets a bit sticky sometimes," John fibbed trying to cover the struggling young man's embarrassment. "Here, let me do it."

With the belt undone, John climbed quickly out of the car, slammed the door shut, and then hurried around to help Sticks. He wasn't quite quick enough though. The poor boy pretty much fell out of the car and then collapsed to the ground where he lay like a pile of dirty rags. With a stifled, horrified cry, John rushed to the boy's aid. He tried to get him to stand but Sticks didn't stir; and this time he wasn't just asleep, he was now fully unconscious.

John wasted no time. In an instant he slammed the passenger door shut and locked the car. He then swept Sticks up into his arms and ran towards the Accident and Emergency entrance. He marvelled at just how little he weighed; clearly a sore foot was the least of the boy's problems.

John burst into the reception area and hurried through to the desk. The receptionist looked up and gave him a small and jaded smile. "Yes?" she said a little brusquely.

"This young man's in a bad way," John said hurriedly. "He just collapsed in the carpark outside. He's very thin and malnourished and I think he's got a lot of other problems too."

"Collapsed you say?"

"Yes, just a few moments ago."

"Right, you'd better bring him straight through."

The woman got to her feet and led John down a short corridor. In no time at all Sticks was taken from him and placed in a cubicle. He was asked a few quick questions before, with many a backward glance, John was led back to the reception area.

"If I can just have some more details?"

John sighed. "There's not much I can tell you, but I'll give you as much info as I know." He glanced back towards the corridor and offered a silent prayer for the poor unfortunate boy.

CHAPTER SEVEN – *"START CHILDREN OFF ON THE WAY THEY SHOULD GO, AND EVEN WHEN THEY ARE OLD THEY WILL NOT TURN FROM IT." (PROVERBS 22:6)*

Sticks – The Third Prayer

It was exactly one year and four days before the anniversary of the soup kitchen's opening, and sixteen-year-old Dean James rested his head back against the car seat's headrest and closed his eyes. His fearful excitement had robbed him of sleep all night, but tired as he was, the knot in his stomach was still too tight to allow him to drift off.

"You tired lad?" the car's driver enquired sympathetically.

"No," Dean replied quietly. "Just thinking."

"Ah, I see. My name's Jim, by the way. What's yours?"

"Sticks."

"Sticks? That's an unusual one."

"Yeah, I know. It's just what everyone calls me."

It was true. He'd been inseparable from his precious drumsticks for the last three years, and somehow the nickname had stuck. Although that nasty piece of work, Wayne, had meant it as an insult, Dean had been proud to adopt it as his name. But then yesterday, Wayne had snapped them in half. He'd also broken Sticks' phone.

"Well I tell you what Sticks, you've got some luck all right. I've never stopped for a hitchhiker before, and the first time I do, he's going to the same place as me."

Jim was right; he *had* been lucky that morning. He'd only walked a mile or so along the A1 before the Ford Mondeo had responded to his outstretched thumb.

"Where are you going to?" Jim had called as he'd leant towards the passenger window.

"A place called Rewford."

The surprise on Jim's face had been comical to behold. "Well blow me down, so am I!"

"So whereabouts in Rewford are you heading for?" Jim asked conversationally as they cruised down the A1.

"Churchill Close; but I'm not sure where it is exactly. My phone got broken before I could look it up on Google Maps."

Jim frowned. "Hmm; Churchill Close. Can't say as I know it." His face suddenly brightened. "Hang on though; there's an estate on the far side of town where all the streets are named after famous people. You know, Victoria Avenue, Montgomery Drive, and the like. I reckon it's probably up there."

"I don't suppose you're going near it, are you?" Sticks asked hopefully.

"Sorry, son; my office is situated about a mile this side of town. That estate's probably a good mile from the far side. You'll still have about four miles to go when I drop you off."

"Oh," Sticks replied in a crestfallen voice.

Jim eyed his passenger thoughtfully. "Tell you what, lad, I'll go past my turning and swing back round on the Frinton road. If I drop you off somewhere around there you can cut through the centre of town. I can't do better than that but at least it'll save you a couple of miles."

"Thanks a lot," Sticks said with genuine gratitude. "I really do appreciate it."

"No problem. Tell you what, you really do look knackered. Knock your seat back and get some sleep for an hour or so."

Sticks smiled and grunted his appreciation. He reached down and located the lever to adjust his seat. Once tipped back, he shut his eyes and dozed, not quite falling into a true sleep. And as he dozed, his mind drifted back, recalling the events that had led him to this most momentous journey in his short life.

Having been abandoned as a toddler he had lived all his life in a Catholic children's home – apart from a couple of short-lived foster homes that is. And it hadn't been a happy childhood in the least. Slight of build with rather pretty features, he'd been badly bullied by some of the older boys. And there'd been other, more sinister problems to deal with. Father Jolly, for instance. Oh, how they'd laughed when he'd introduced himself at the compulsory Sunday school; oh, how he'd laughed along with them. It turned out that Jolly was indeed his real name; and it suited him. With his twinkling blue eyes and beaming, red-cheeked face, he really was a happy-looking fellow. He had a great sense of humour too, and he made the staid and boring Sunday school something to really look forward to. And when he'd asked twelve-year-old Sticks to stay behind one day, the young lad had been over the moon. That had been the first of the innumerable incidents of sexual abuse perpetrated on him by the jolly Father Jolly.

He had profoundly mixed and contradictory feelings about Father Jolly. There was a deep disgust, but there was excitement too; there was loathing but there was also love. The degenerate priest had made a lonely, rejected boy feel special and wanted. But Sticks' overriding feelings were ones of guilt. He felt guilty because it had been sordid and wrong; but he also felt guilty because of the feelings of pleasure and love it had given him. Emotionally and spiritually, his relationship with Father Jolly had torn his soul apart. Not that this had anything to do with his absconding from the home now. No, this was the culmination of a series of events that had been set in motion almost a year ago.

It had all started when he'd seen a feature on the news about an adopted girl finding her real mother. It had led to a joyful reunion with many hugs and happy tears. Apparently, there was now a law that allowed the child to trace their birthmother. It had moved him immensely, so much so that he'd immediately gone to see Andrew, the home's supervisor, and had asked how he was to begin the process. Andrew's reaction had stunned him.

"Don't be stupid, Dean," he'd said with a sneer that Sticks had probably imagined. "If your mother wanted to be found she'd have been in contact with you long before now. And anyway, you have to be eighteen before you can even think about tracing her."

And that should have been the end of it, but Sticks was now like a dog with a bone. He'd pestered everyone. Nuns, teachers, cooks, assistants – just about every adult he came into contact with. Then, two weeks ago he'd been outside Andrew's office when he'd overheard Jane, one of the assistants, talking to him about it.

"...won't let it go. Frankly, it's getting far too embarrassing to put up with."

"I understand what you're saying; and you're not the first to complain."

"Well, what are we going to do about it?"

"I don't know," Andrew had sighed. "The boy's obsessed."

"He could do with a psychiatrist, if you ask me."

"Counselling certainly is one option," Andrew had conceded thoughtfully.

"He needs something," Jane had replied harshly. "Can you imagine what would happen if he actually managed to find her?"

"Oh, I wouldn't worry about that. I looked into it a couple of months ago and there's no chance of him tracing her. She's since married and moved far, far away. Without going through the proper, official channels, even a persistent little so-and-so like Dean will get nowhere."

"*You* found her," Jane had countered disturbingly.

"Ah, but that's me," Andrew had replied, sounding far too smug. "I have my own special connections."

At that point Sticks had slipped away with a plan formulating in his mind.

Later that night, he'd crept out of bed and had broken into Andrew's office. Neither the lock on the door nor the one to the filing cabinet had been a problem for Sticks. Lock picking was a skill many of the home's kids had acquired from the more 'troubled' children resident there. Even so, after a long, torch lit search through the many files in the cabinet, he'd had no luck. When he'd eventually found his own file, nowhere in it was there any mention of his real mother – or his obsession with her. In fact, there was almost nothing in it at all. And anyway, Andrew's enquiries with his 'connections' would probably have all been made by telephone.

He'd flashed his torch around the room and the beam had fallen onto the screen of the computer.

Could he have corresponded by email? If so, without the correct passwords, those emails might just as well have been on the moon.

Sticks had grinned widely; he *did* have the correct passwords. Several times he'd watched as Andrew had gone into the computer, and Sticks had a very good memory indeed. Soon he'd been sitting in the supervisor's chair, scrolling through a vast list of Andrew's private emails. They told him absolutely nothing other than the fact that the supervisor needed to clear out his inbox more often.

Hugely disappointed, he'd been about to shut the computer down when a new thought had struck him. He'd come out of Andrew's private settings and had searched the home's official database. It took a while, but he'd eventually found the records of every one of the home's 'inmates' as they saw themselves.

Dean James, the file read. It gave his date of birth, sex, and all the other irrelevant information but there were a couple of separate folders contained within the file. And in one of these he'd struck pay dirt. There was a screenshot of an email from someone he couldn't remember, but it had read:

"Andrew. While I understand your concerns please put your mind at ease. I've made discreet enquiries and I can assure you that the boy's mother's identity is perfectly safe – although quite why the boy's surname wasn't changed, I

have no idea. It most definitely should have been! At least she now has a new name, and she has moved to a location far away from you. In fact, Mrs Hatcher lives in Rewford, which is a good two hundred miles away!"

With trembling hands Sticks had shut the computer down and had crept quietly back to his room, making sure to have covered his tracks. Why on Earth the old fool had been stupid enough to leave such sensitive information in the file, he couldn't imagine. "The stupid prat's gonna regret it now though," Sticks had thought. It never once crossed his mind that Andrew had kept it there for Sticks' own benefit – to save him the immense hassle of the process when he turned eighteen.

It had then taken a bare three days of searching Facebook to find his mother. Her first name was Julie – at least he was ninety percent certain that it was her. She'd even posted a selfie standing beside her front door with the number fifteen clearly visible. And another photo had revealed the name of her street. He'd been tempted to send a friend request, but good sense had prevailed and he'd resisted the temptation. But he could watch her; and at least in some vague and distant way, he could be part of her life.

But then last night there'd been the fight with Wayne. Sticks had been sitting in the common room, scrolling through Julie's Facebook page on his phone. In his other hand he'd been tapping his thigh with his precious drumsticks.

"What you looking at?" Wayne had asked, snatching the phone from Sticks' hand. "Who's this tart then, your girlfriend?"

It was the last straw. Sticks had been subjected to this animal's bullying for the last time. He would be his victim no longer. Howling like a madman, he'd hurled himself at the brawny seventeen-year-old. Such was the surprise of the attack, he'd managed to land a good solid punch on Wayne's ugly, brutish face. The seven other kids in the room had cheered and shrieked, egging the two combatants on. As Wayne had staggered back, Sticks' phone had flown through the air and into the wall with such force that the case had broken and the screen had cracked. Sticks had then tried to jab his opponent in the face with a drumstick, but although his opponent was a goliath, Sticks was no David.

Fortunately though, the unequal contest was ended before Wayne could inflict any real retaliatory damage. One of the nuns had come running in to see what all the noise was about; and Sister Grace was a big powerful woman, so she easily pulled the two apart. But not before Wayne had managed to snap the precious drumsticks in half. Both boys had then been sent to their rooms in disgrace. The look Wayne had shot Sticks promised savage revenge at the nearest possible opportunity.

So Sticks had decided to run away the next morning. There were only three days of school left before half-term anyway, so the hue and cry shouldn't go up too soon – or so he hoped. Tomorrow he would go and find his mother, and surely once she heard his tale, she would be bound to take pity on him. Perhaps there would be a tearful welcome, just like the one he'd seen on the telly.

So now here he was, wafting down the A1 on his way to meet her; and he couldn't wait to see the surprise on her face when he did.

CHAPTER EIGHT – *"THOUGH MY FATHER AND MOTHER FORSAKE ME, THE LORD WILL RECEIVE ME." (PSALM 27:10)*

Sticks – The Third Prayer

"**T**here you go son, this is it."

"Thanks, Jim," Sticks said a little absently as he looked through the car windows at their surroundings.

"Don't mention it. Now if you go down that road on your left, it swings round towards the centre of town; but you don't want to go all the way into the town centre. About half a mile along, there'll be a turning on your left called Jubilee Road. That takes you right up to the estate you want. It's a bit of a climb though; uphill all the way."

Sticks turned and looked at his benefactor, actually registering his appearance properly for the first time. He was perhaps in his late thirties or early forties with a handsome, friendly face. His brown hair was neatly cut and immaculately combed. His plain, dark blue suit and crisp white shirt contrasted well with his brightly patterned, red tie. He was probably some kind of executive, Sticks decided. The Mondeo was top of the range too.

"You really have been most kind."

"You won't say that if you get all the way up to the top of the hill and Churchill Close isn't there," laughed Jim. "If you meet someone on the way, it might be a good idea to ask for directions."

"I will," Sticks replied earnestly.

Then without another word he climbed out of the car and shut the door. After they shared a cheery wave, the car accelerated away. Sticks watched it go admiringly. It was indeed a nice car; very classy for a mere Ford. Absently he wondered what trim level the odd fish shape on the back signified.

He took a deep breath and then started off down the road Jim had pointed to. Carefully, he checked the street name of every turning he passed until after about half a mile, he found the one he wanted. It was exactly where his generous lift-provider had said it would be. Unfortunately, it also looked just as steep a climb as he'd warned it would be. What Jim hadn't told him though, was just how well-to-do an area this was. The houses were large, mostly detached and set well back from the road. From what he'd seen on Facebook, his mother's house was certainly not in as affluent an area as this. Sticks looked around for someone to ask directions from, but for as far as he could see, there was no one about.

"Oh well," he muttered to himself. "Only one way to find out."

With an equal measure of dread and excitement gripping his soul, he started on the long walk up the hill. It was fairly mild for an October day, with an overcast sky that threatened rain. Sticks was soon starting to sweat, but he was stubbornly reluctant to remove his blue parka. It was wonderfully warm and waterproof, and a real hindrance when performing gruelling exercise such as this. But it had been a surprise gift from Jessie, one of the few assistants he'd really liked. She'd only been at the home for a few short months before she'd suddenly left. It seemed the coat had been a parting gift, and he now treasured it nearly as much as he'd treasured his drumsticks.

He seemed to be about half way up the interminably long hill when he met the only passer-by. She was a well-dressed attractive woman, perhaps in her early thirties. Sticks saw her as she emerged from a very expensive-looking house about thirty yards away on the other side of the road. She then started hurrying down the hill towards him. Quickly the boy crossed the road so as to intercept her.

"Excuse me," he called politely while she was still a short distance away. "I'm looking for Churchill Close."

The woman gave him a snooty, disapproving look. "Hmm..." she said eying him up and down distastefully. "Yes," she said at last in a very posh voice. "It's on the *estate* at the top of the hill." From the way she'd said 'estate', Sticks got the impression she considered it to be one of those deprived sink estates he'd often seen on the telly. Not exactly what he'd seen on Facebook either.

"Thanks," he said in a tone that made it clear he found her as distasteful as she obviously found him.

The woman tutted loudly and then pushed past him.

'Manners maketh man' was a line from Sticks' favourite film, but clearly money did not maketh manners.

In the end, the estate was rather nice. It was one of those newly built, modern estates with identical, compact, semi-detached houses. They all had a tiny garage attached – barely big enough for a small family car – with a very short drive in front of that. Each had a tiny patch of grass that served as a front garden with a short path leading to the front door. Not a single house had a fence of any kind. The whole estate had a clean and modern feel that was totally devoid of character. Sticks liked it a lot.

It was not a particularly big estate, but Sticks knew it might take him a while to find the road he was looking for. Then, just minutes later he spotted someone. Again, it was a woman, but this one was a little younger and looked far more down to Earth. She emerged from her front door opposite him and started to get into her almost new Kia Picanto.

"Churchill Close?" he called without bothering to cross the road.

"That way," the woman shouted back with a big friendly smile. "Second left, third right." She then jumped into the little car, started it, and backed it off the tiny drive with indecent haste. She then shot off up the narrow street far too fast for such roads as these. She was clearly in a very big hurry indeed.

"Thanks," he muttered to the rapidly disappearing car, before adding a sarcastic, "Drive careful." Even so, he was more than a little impressed by her turn of speed.

With his inner turmoil mounting, he followed the 'fast lady's' directions and soon arrived at his destination – far too soon in fact. He stood hesitating in front of the short path, his heart pounding wildly in his chest. It was a twitch of the curtain that motivated him in the end. He realised that he must look conspicuously menacing just standing there looking at the house.

He took a deep breath, marched up the short path, and rang the doorbell. It was one of those musical ones and it played the first few bars of a tune he knew.

Ding dong, ding dong; your head's gone wrong.

Three screws are loose; your head's no use.

Unasked and unwanted, the comical words accompanied the tune in his mind, mocking the gravity of the occasion. Then came the approaching footsteps and the distorted figure of a woman became visible through the two frosted panels of the door. And then it opened.

She looked much younger than she'd appeared on her Facebook page, although from what he knew she was actually thirty-two. Her blonde hair was cut in a fashionably short style that suited her pretty, elfin features. But seeing her in the flesh made him all the more certain of her identity. He'd seen her eyes and mouth reflected in the bathroom mirror every morning.

"Hello mum," he said, his voice shaking with emotion. "I'm your son, Dean."

Julie Hatcher froze. The blood drained from her face and her eyes widened. Strained seconds passed; and then she spoke.

"F*** off!" she hissed vehemently and then slammed the door shut.

Her words struck Sticks like a physical blow. Although his body didn't flinch, his heart was crushed as if from a savage blow by a sledgehammer. It was now his turn to stand frozen and immobile; but his own paralysis knew no end. He had no idea how long he'd been standing there when eventually the front door was thrown open again.

"If you don't clear off, I'm calling the police!" his estranged mother threatened fiercely.

Sticks gawped at her for a moment before, as if in a trance, he turned and shuffled away.

"And don't come back," Julie Hatcher called after him. She then looked up and down the close to see if anyone had heard her before once again, she slammed the front door shut.

* * *

Sticks sat numbly on the park bench. Unseeingly, he watched the children at play, safe and secure in the chain-link fenced compound a few feet away. They laughed and shouted merrily as they chased each other around the miniature wooden fort with its own little slide. A just a few yards from them, a mother was pushing her little girl on a swing. It was as idyllic a scene of family happiness as you could want to see.

Just what had attracted Sticks to the park was a mystery. In a stunned, hopeless dream he'd retraced his steps to the bottom of the hill. Without thinking he'd then turned left towards the town centre. He'd only gone about two hundred yards when he'd heard the children. Somehow the sound had penetrated the stunned blankness of his mind, and had drawn him to it like the song of a siren.

The park entrance was located a few yards along a road on his left, and without thought or reason, he'd soon found himself sitting on that bench. Time passed; the children left with their mothers; the light faded as night closed in, and still Sticks didn't move. The sky cleared and the few visible stars shone bleakly down, as cold as his heart and as faint as its beating. Midnight came and went, but still he sat there.

Eventually though, his thoughts began to return, and with them came the despair. He now had nothing. No mother, no hope, and not even a home. Or did he? There was nothing stopping him from hitching a lift back to the home, was there? True, he'd been really lucky to get a lift the whole way here, but...

He snorted bitterly. He knew in his heart of hearts that the chances of repeating such amazing luck were nil. It would probably take him days to get back there. There was only one chance: to hop a train. It would take some doing, but there must surely be a way of getting on and avoiding being caught. And if he *was* caught, so what? What could they do, fine him? He was legally a kid, and he had no parents they could chase for the money.

Slowly, he rose from the bench and made his way through the dark towards the entrance. He headed in the direction of the town centre again, listening to the quiet of the morning's early hours. He would get to the station and wait for it to open. If he could get onto the platform now, all the better. But where exactly was the station? He almost laughed a few minutes later when, just as approached the town he spotted a sign pointing the way. Luck again?

Five minutes later and he was there. It was locked but it looked as though it would be easy enough to shin over the fence. But just as he was about to start climbing, he stopped still. What exactly was he going back to? Wayne's bullying? The coldness of some of the assistants? The apparently fake piety of the nuns? Father Jolly? The degenerate priest hadn't touched him for months now – he'd probably found someone younger – but just seeing him there every week was always a twist of the knife. And to go back to the Bible lessons and services. The Holy Trinity, Holy Mary, Mother of God, Saint this and Saint that. No, it was too much. God was nothing more than a sick joke! And he would definitely be in big trouble for absconding.

He turned away and resumed his walk towards town, not sure of what he would do when he got there. He was lucky enough to have ten pounds in his pocket, but that wasn't going to keep him going for long. Even cheap sandwiches would eat into it really fast. There was nothing for it, he would have to beg. He'd seen it on the news; and if the winos and druggies could get enough to keep them going, then surely the price of a MacDonald's would be no problem.

He'd not gone far when he started to see shops. Unlike many places, Rewford still had a decent High Street experience for its citizens, so they were nice shops. Very nice, apart from one small and empty one incongruously situated amongst the others. Curious, Sticks stopped and looked in the window. In the soft light of the streetlamps he saw a little poster.

Free soup Kitchen 10 PM Market Square.
Open every night from Saturday 20th October.
Hot food and drink for those in need.

It seemed he wouldn't have to beg too hard after all.

CHAPTER NINE – *"THE LORD IS NEAR TO THOSE WHO HAVE A BROKEN HEART, AND SAVES SUCH AS HAVE A CONTRITE SPIRIT." (PSALM 34:18)*

Sticks – The Third Prayer

L ife on the streets was much harder than Sticks had anticipated. His ten pounds had kept him fed for the few days until the soup kitchen opened, but certainly not so much as to keep hunger at bay. And even once the nightly meal became available, it still wasn't sufficient to keep him properly fed. And then there was the cold. Although it was only autumn – a warm one at that – and his parka was a good coat, nothing could have prepared him for the chill of the early hours. After the fifth night, he could take it no longer. He had no family, no friends, and no hope. He had an overwhelming feeling that his life was over; and if it was over, why keep on living? But how to end it was a problem. A news story flashed into his head. A reporter was interviewing witnesses after someone had thrown themselves under a train. As he sat huddled in a shop doorway in the chill pre-dawn, he resolved to end it all the same way.

He got to his feet and started trudging through the empty town. There was a ghostly, eerie feel to the light from the streetlamps that somehow suited his mood. A sudden thought brought him up short. It was far too early. There would be no trains running yet – precious few at least. He would be better off waiting until later. He looked around for somewhere he could pass the time in reasonable comfort, and his eyes fell on the semi-circle of the bandstand. Just where it abutted the end wall of a row of shops, it formed a shallow niche behind a bench. His mind numb from despair, he walked mechanically over to it and hunkered down.

It was a great little spot. If only he'd noticed it before he might have been more comfortable – a little bit, anyway. He rested his head back against the wall and within just a few minutes, his exhausted eyes closed and he fell asleep.

He didn't notice the board being pulled open from inside the bandstand just a few feet away. His eyes remained firmly closed as the figure of a man crawled out from the small gap it provided. Jerry immediately noticed him though; and he recognised him from the soup kitchen too. The ex-soldier knelt looking at him for a few moments and then smiled to himself. He turned back to the gap and crawled halfway in, clearly reaching for something. He re-emerged with his sleeping bag which he gently laid over the boy's legs, covering him up to his waist. Sticks didn't stir. Jerry then replaced the board and squatted beside the sleeping boy, mainly to guard his precious sleeping bag.

Not until almost ten o'clock did Sticks' eyes flicker open. It took a few puzzled seconds for him to remember where he was and for his eyes to focus on the man squatting at his side. Jerry was staring hungrily at the chip shop; it was not yet open but they were obviously almost ready to unlock the door. A flash of recognition crossed Sticks' mind. He'd seen the man in front of him at the soup kitchen although he didn't know his name. It was then that he noticed the sleeping bag.

"What...?

"Hello kid," Jerry said as he realised Sticks was awake. "Sleep well?"

Sticks blinked uncomprehendingly. "What's this?" he said lifting the corner of his warm covering.

"It's a bleedin' sleeping bag," Jerry replied with a scornful snort. "And since you're awake, I'll have it back."

"Oh, of course." Sticks got to his feet and passed it to the stern-faced Good Samaritan.

Jerry quickly rolled it up then nodded at Sticks. "Good luck, kid. Take my advice, find something to keep you warm." Then without waiting for a reply, he marched quickly away.

Sticks watched him go. "Yeah, thanks for the advice," he muttered bitterly. A moment later the despair once again flooded his soul in a black cloud of hopelessness. His resolve to end it all returned all the more solidly, in spite of the random act of kindness he'd just been shown. And now the time was ripe to put his plan into action.

In a bitter dream he continued his journey toward his rendezvous with oblivion. He saw without seeing the growing number of visitors to the town centre, almost bumping into one particular lady who crossed his path. He muttered an automatic, "Sorry," then gawped at her as she pushed her way into a small charity shop. She was holding several extremely large, overstuffed carrier bags, but what had really caught his eye was the item under her arm. Even though covered by its protective case, it was unmistakably a tightly rolled up sleeping bag. And since it was going into a charity shop, it would be cheap – or would it? This particular charity – something to do with hearts – was never *that* cheap. He put his hand in his pocket and pulled out the remnants of his meagre takings from yesterday's begging. A measly £1.45. That would never be enough. With a heavy sigh he decided to continue his fateful appointment with eternity.

He blinked in amazement when he found himself inside the shop. The lady had placed everything on the counter and the shop assistant – a weasel faced, middle aged woman – was starting to pull things out of the carrier bags. A suit, a bright blue coat, and a couple of shirts had already emerged for examination; and there beside them was the object of his desire.

"They were my late husband's," the lady was saying. "All the best quality."

"How...how much for the sleeping bag?" he stammered quietly.

The woman behind the counter gave him a withering look. "It's not for sale," she said coldly. "Everything needs to be logged in first."

The lady who was making the donation turned and looked at him sternly. "Why is that, young man?" she asked in a clipped, upper-class tone that nonetheless held an underlying compassion. "Are you going camping?" She looked very strange to Sticks. She was tall, in her late sixties or early seventies, and obviously belonged to the higher echelons of society. Yet she was dressed in an old, dark-green waxed cotton jacket under which was a thick, loose-knit brown jumper. Her long grey hair was tied back into a single ponytail, held by a simple black band.

"I...I just get cold at night."

The lady's expression softened very slightly; at first glance, her dark brown eyes appeared hard and severe, but behind all that there was a hint of sympathy. "I bet you do," she said in a crisp and authoritative voice that matched her abrupt manner.

"I...I've got one pound forty-five," sticks said hopefully."

"I've already told you it's not for sale," the shop woman stated emphatically.

"Oh, come now," the lady chided. "I'm sure we can come to an accommodation for the boy."

"It's all got to be logged in," the weasel-faced woman repeated.

"Then I'll take the sleeping bag back; then you won't need to log it in." The lady's clipped voice now carried a distinctly frosty tone.

"You can't take it back once you've donated it," the woman replied. Despite her firm words however, her resolve was clearly beginning to waver under the lady's icy glare.

"You *will* hand it back, and you will hand it back *now!*"

"But...erm... Oh, very well!" The flustered woman picked up the sleeping bag by its cover's carry-strap and thrust it towards the lady who'd donated it.

"Thank you," the lady replied in a voice that could freeze salt. She then turned to Sticks. "How much did you say you have there, young man?" she asked brusquely. Her frosty contempt had now been replaced by a crisp, business-like manner.

"One pound forty-five."

"Ridiculous," she snapped. "This is a top-quality item. I can't sell it to you for less than thirty-five pounds." She swung around to the shop woman. "Pen; paper," she snapped at her.

The woman was about to argue but under the withering blast of the lady's glare, she hurriedly obliged. The lady then wrote something on the paper and then offered the pen to Sticks. "Here you are boy; sign it."

Sticks gulped and then moved over to the counter. In neat, well-formed capital letters she had printed:

FOR THE SALE OF ONE BLACKTHORN
SLEEPING BAG:
I.O.U. £35.00

SIGNED:

In a daze, Sticks took the pen and bent over the paper.

"Just a scribble will do," the lady said briskly.

Obediently, Sticks did just that and then made to hand the pen back to her.

"That's *my* pen," the shop woman said indignantly.

Ignoring her, the lady took the pen from him and then handed him the sleeping bag. "There you go boy, it's yours. Look after it; you've just paid a lot of money for it."

Blankly, Sticks took the bag and looked into her face. It wore a hard, stern expression; but was that a friendly twinkle behind her severe and unyielding eyes? "Th...thank you," he managed to stammer.

She acknowledged his gratitude with a sharp nod. "Well go on lad; off you go."

Unsure of what else to do, Sticks turned and fled from the shop. Behind him the weasel-faced shop woman picked up the note to read what was on it.

"That's mine!" the lady said, snatching it out of the woman's hand. She then tore it up and put the pieces into her pocket. "Right then," she barked, handing the woman back her pen. "Where were we?"

* * *

Although the sleeping bag certainly made his life more bearable, and the act of overwhelming generosity had dispelled his suicidal thoughts, Sticks' overall condition still deteriorated over the next few months. Winter took its toll and there were now more and more rough sleepers in Rewford. There were even a couple of women – one of whom was certainly mad. Their gradually increasing numbers had made the begging less and less rewarding. By the time spring came around there seemed to be at least fifteen, or even twenty – a lot for such a modest-sized town. He was finding it almost impossible to glean enough to feed himself, for in truth, he wasn't a very accomplished beggar. By early summer, the situation was becoming critical. He was dirty, dishevelled, and unbelievably thin. Reverend John had tried to help him of course, but the sight of

John's dog collar brought back too many traumatic memories for Sticks.

It was after one such attempt at an intervention that Sticks finally broke down completely.

"You know son," John said quietly. "I usually find prayer helps when things get really bad. I'm happy to pray with you, if you want to try." The Rev put a sympathetically encouraging hand on his shoulder; but the touch of a clergyman's hand was just too much for him to bear. The traumatized boy flinched away from it and then ran off into the night.

Sometime later, Sticks found himself standing in the park beside the enclosed children's playground. He could just see the swings silhouetted against the streetlights outside the park. The memory of the giggling little girl being pushed by her mother flashed into his mind; and with that came thoughts of his own mother's betrayal. The cruel obscenity she'd spat at him still cut him to the core. The unbearable iniquity of it all crashed down on him, crushing his soul into a pit of hopeless misery. For the first time in many years he began to cry. At first with stinging tears of self-pity, but then the leak became a flood, and then the flood became a tidal wave. His heaving sobs grew so painfully violent, it seemed he must surely crack a rib.

Memories of Father Jolly and the cold, uncaring nuns appeared in his mind. He remembered the interminable church services he was forced to endure – and he wasn't even a proper catholic! Those he perceived to be wicked had continually preached about their God; so all the terrible things he'd been force to undergo were all God's work!

"God!" he cried when at last he could breathe. "Why? What did I do to deserve this? I hate you, I hate you, I hate you; I HATE YOU!"

After screaming out his bitterness and anger with the Almighty, he lay down on the grass and curled into a foetal ball.

He lay there for some time, crying softly, his mind a sea of bleak and painful torment.

But then an image of Reverend Winters came to mind. He was so unlike Father Jolly. He was unselfishly caring, never asking anything in return for his kindness. And there were others. There was Jim, who'd picked him up on the A1 and had brought him all the way to Rewford; there was that lady who'd pretended to sell him his sleeping bag; even Jerry had shown him kindness in an offhand kind of way. He didn't know about the lady and Jerry, but he'd since discovered that the fish on the back of Jim's car meant that he was a Christian just like the Rev. So who was God really? A wicked sadist or a loving comforter? Was he Jolly's God, or the Rev's God? But if he *was* the Rev's God then...

"I'm sorry, God. I'm sorry, I'm sorry, I'm sorry."

Then he began to pray. It was a real, heartfelt, desperate prayer. But there were almost no words, just an unbearable, aching cry for help. Slowly, his weeping ceased, and he fell into a deep and untroubled sleep.

CHAPTER TEN – *"THE WICKED ONE LIES IN WAIT FOR THE RIGHTEOUS AND SEEKS TO KILL HIM;" (PSALM 37:32)*

Sticks – The Third Prayer

It was now the first week in July and although Sticks' physical condition was still much the same, emotionally he seemed to be in a far better place. When he'd woken up on the morning after his meltdown, there'd been a change within him. A subtle, almost intangible change, but nonetheless profound in spite of its apparent lack of substance. For some reason he didn't feel quite so alone.

Now, two weeks later he was walking through the plush, indoor market near the town centre when he was surprised by a firm hand grasping his shoulder from behind.

"Hello boy," came a clipped woman's voice. "I thought I recognised you."

He turned to see the kind, strange lady from the charity shop. She was looking at him with a stern, unsmiling expression.

"Well don't just stand there gawping lad. In polite society it's expected to exchange a friendly greeting with another."

"Erm... hello."

"That's better." She glanced at the sleeping bag which was tucked under his arm along with his parka. "Looking after it I trust?"

"What? Oh yes; yes of course I am."

"Good." Her severe expression then softened very slightly. "Hmm. You look like you need a little company. Come on boy, let's go and have a chat."

Sticks was horrified. "No, I can't. It's nice of you but I've..."

"What; got things to do? Don't be ridiculous. Come along with me now, boy." She took a firm hold of his shoulders and turned him around. "This way." She propelled him along by placing a hand in the middle of his back and giving him a gentle shove. And since she was pushing him in the same direction he was originally going, it was impossible for him to resist.

Under the lady's strong leadership, the pair were soon out into the warm afternoon sunshine. Although Sticks had a serious urge to bolt and run away, such was the lady's hold over him – one that was more than just physical – he had no choice other than to acquiesce. She led him all the way back into town and, to his great surprise, all the way up to the bandstand.

"Sit," she said pointing to the seat opposite the chip shop. Two people were already sitting there, but after an intimidating glare from the lady, they immediately got up and moved away. Instinctively Sticks obeyed her instruction and she sat down beside him. "So how are things going?" she asked a little more softly.

"All right, I suppose."

She eyed him up and down. "Hmm," she said dubiously. "It looks like it." There was no denying his obviously parlous state. "You look like you could do with a portion of chips. "What do you say lad; a quick bite while we chat?"

How could he refuse? He was starving. "Erm... I'd love to but...but I haven't got any money on me."

"Don't be foolish. I invited you so it's my treat. You can pay next time."

"Erm... All right then."

"Right; sit there, I'll be back in a jiffy." She got up and was about to walk away when she suddenly stopped and gave him one of her coldly commanding stares. "And do stop all that 'erm' business. It makes you sound like the village idiot."

"Erm...okay; sorry."

With an exasperated shake of her head, she crossed the road and entered the chip shop. A few minutes later she was back, juggling heroically with two white paper-wrapped parcels – one considerably larger than the other – along with two cans of coke.

"Here you are, boy," she said handing him the larger package. "Eat and enjoy."

Sticks' eyes widened in wonder when he opened the paper wrapping to reveal, not just a very large portion of chips, but a nice piece of battered cod, a meat pie, and two battered sausages. "Wow!" he exclaimed, unable to believe what he was seeing.

The lady frowned. "Hmm; yes, I'm sorry about that. I'd forgotten to ask what you wanted so I brought something of everything they had left."

"It's...I'm..." He turned and looked into her face. "Thank you," he breathed with tears of gratitude stinging his eyes."

"You're welcome. Now eat up; and if you can't eat it all in one go, I'm sure you'll find cold chips will still be tasty tomorrow."

Sticks nodded and then launched a mighty assault on the food. The lady watched him for a moment and let slip a brief smile that revealed an immense well of warmth and compassion. But a fraction of a second later it was gone and her expression returned to its usual one of stern brevity. She unwrapped her own food – just a small portion of chips – and began to eat.

"My name's Catherine," she said between mouthfuls. "Cath, to my friends. And since this is an official dinner date, we are now firm friends and that is what you will call me. What's yours?"

"Sticks," came the muffled reply.

"I'm sorry boy, I can't understand you with your mouth full. Has no one taught you any manners?"

Sticks hurriedly swallowed his chips. "Sorry. It's Sticks; my name's Sticks."

"If you say it is. Well then 'Sticks', I can tell from your accent that you're not local, so what brought you to Rewford?"

Sticks froze. He stared into her face unsure of what to say. He almost blurted out the truth but the enormity of it all stayed his tongue. "Just things," he said at last.

"Ah yes," Cath said sagely. "Things. There's nothing quite so daunting as things. But apart from the 'things', how are you managing? Not too well by the look of you."

"I'm doing okay."

"Hah!" Cath exclaimed. "If you're doing okay then I must be a billionairess."

Sticks frowned at her, but the twinkle in her eye soon brought a smile to his lips. "Oh, all right, perhaps not quite okay."

"There, that's better. There should always be honesty between friends." And then she launched into a rapid, staccato, one-sided conversation that to Sticks' relief, left few gaps for him to join in. And with another wave of gratitude he realised that this was deliberate. This wonderfully paradoxical woman was intentionally doing it to make him feel unpressured. There was no room for awkward silences.

Eventually, the size of Sticks' meal beat him. He sat back and blew out his cheeks with satisfaction. He picked up his can of coke and finished the last few drops.

"Right then Sticks," Cath said in a brusque, matter of fact voice. "This is how it's going to be; I'm away on business tomorrow, but the day after I'll be here in town. If you happen to be waiting here at two o'clock, you can return the compliment and buy me lunch."

"But...but I can't afford..."

"Then you'll have to share mine," she said patting his knee. "Well I'll be off now. Keep your leftovers for tomorrow and hopefully I'll see you here at two o'clock the day after tomorrow." She screwed up her wrapping paper and handed it to Sticks. "You can do the washing up – and make sure it goes in a bin and not on the floor."

Sticks grinned. "I will. And thanks."

Cath nodded. "My pleasure. And sticks, while it's polite to say 'thank you', it is bad manners to repeat it too often." She shook her head in dismay. "I'm going to have a lot to do teaching you some proper etiquette." Then without another word she was gone.

"I thought a goodbye would be good manners," Sticks muttered with amused irony. He then carefully rewrapped his leftovers and made his way back to the doorway where he regularly begged for spare change. But he made sure to deposit the empty cans and Cath's paper in a bin on the way.

Two days later, Sticks was once again sitting by the bandstand, and true to her word, right at the stroke of two, Cath arrived. Once again, she treated him to a huge meal, and once again she launched into her one-sided conversation. At first Sticks was a little embarrassed by her generosity, but her brisk, matter-of-fact manner soon made it seem more a force of nature than an act of charity. One might just as well be embarrassed by a brief burst of sunshine on an overcast day.

And that was how it went on for exactly five weeks and two days. Three or four times a week they met up by the bandstand where Cath treated him to a huge feast. Slowly, she left more and more pauses in her monologue, and slowly – oh so very slowly – Sticks began to open up. The boy's happiest moment came when she took him to the town's large car park for 'a surprise'. She led him to the public toilets and stopped outside the door marked, 'Disabled Only'. He knew for a fact that the door was always locked and could only be opened by a special key given to those who needed it. But then with a laugh that amazed Sticks more than anything, Cath produced just such a key.

"It was my husband's," she explained with a wicked grin as she unlocked the door. She then propelled him through it and once inside she snicked the lock across and then started to fill the small sink with warm water.

"Why are we in here?" Sticks asked with a puzzled frown.

Cath made no reply but once the sink was filled to her satisfaction, she tore off a large length of the blue paper toweling, screwed it up into a large ball, and dipped into the water. Then to sticks' horror she whirled around and pounced on him, rubbing the soaking paper around his face.

At first angry and terrified, Stick tried to fight her off, but after a matter of moments the ridiculous comedy of the situation became too much. Soon he was in fits of laughter as Cath tried to wash the filth from the lad's face and hands. The boy's attempts to evade the impromptu flannel became more and more ludicrous, even drawing a few chuckles from Cath. Eventually though, she was able to stand back and admire her handiwork.

"There; much better. Now we just need to comb your hair." This of course proved a much more unpleasant ordeal. Over the many months on the streets his hair had grown matted and long. He tried to escape, but once Cath's normal stern and commanding mien returned, he had no option but to submit to the torture of her six-inch, man's comb. When the pair finally left the disabled toilet, Sticks looked a different boy. Still dishevelled and scruffy, but a thousand times more presentable.

Over the weeks his condition continued to improve and his relationship with Cath grew stronger and closer with every 'lunch date'. He'd not even baulked when she'd mentioned her church. It wasn't exactly an invitation to go with her; but it let him know that he'd be welcome to join her if he so desired. There is no telling to what happy ending it could have led, had it not been for that fateful day in August.

There was a jaunty spring in his step as he marched happily along Low Road on his way to the bandstand. This part of town was notable for bric-a-brac shops and clothes stores. He liked to look into some of the menswear shops and dream that one day he too could look as smart as some of the shop dummies. But he wasn't looking in any shops at the moment. His thoughts were fixed firmly on fish and chips and on the best friend he'd ever had in his short, unhappy life.

But then he stopped dead. The blood drained from his face and his veins turned to ice. For there in front of him was Julie Hatcher with her husband, Gary – his step-father. They were standing on the pavement in front of him, arm in arm and laughing happily as they chatted with another smiling couple. But it wasn't seeing his mother that affected him so; it was her huge, swollen belly that was the knife in his soul. And he could clearly read her lips as she affectionately patted her bump and said, "Three weeks." That was the moment when the knife not only twisted, it rent his soul asunder. How could she hate him so, but feel such love for his yet-to-be-born sibling?

Suddenly, he spun on his heels and fled to a small dark alleyway he knew. And there he crouched, eyes closed and numb with a bitter pain greater than any he'd known before.

"See you," came a nearby voice with a heavy Scottish accent. "You appear to be in need of something to help you through the day. How about a wee freebie? You know, just to see what's what."

CHAPTER ELEVEN – *"LET YOUR LAUGHTER BE TURNED TO MOURNING AND YOUR JOY TO GLOOM." (JAMES 4:9)*

Sticks – The Third Prayer

John glanced at his watch. He'd been at the hospital over an hour now. Although Anne had been understanding when he'd phoned to tell her that he'd be a while, there was a limit as to how far he could push her patience. The soup kitchen would be wrapping up soon, and it was too much to expect her to help put everything away. He sighed and got to his feet, debating with himself whether to inform the receptionist that he was leaving. He supposed he better had. After all, he was sitting in the front row just a few steps away from the desk. It would only take a moment.

Just then he saw a white-coated doctor emerge from the corridor down which John had taken Sticks earlier. With mounting trepidation John watched as the doctor approached the reception desk. His expression was one that John had seen many times in his years as a minister. His stomach lurched when the doctor spoke to the girl and she pointed in his direction. It lurched again when the white-coated man walked solemnly across towards him.

"Reverend Winters? I'm Doctor Gibson. Shall we sit a moment?"

John complied then asked the dreaded question: "How is the boy?"

"I'm afraid it's bad news. I'm sorry to tell you that your friend never regained consciousness. He passed away about twenty minutes ago"

John felt as though he'd been slapped. He took a deep breath and forced himself to remain calm. "Do you know what was wrong with him?"

Doctor Gibson sighed heavily. "I'm afraid the exact cause of death would require an autopsy. We do know that he was dehydrated and severely malnourished. His foot was very badly infected and his other foot was likely to go the same way. We couldn't even remove his socks; the skin had begun to grow over them. If I were the type to make guesses however, I'd say it was probably heart failure. It could be that he had a pre-existing heart condition. If that were so, along with all his other problems, it could simply have let go."

"I see." John paused for a moment and the doctor gave him the time to gather his thoughts. "I know the poor boy had a lot going against him," he eventually said. "He's been sleeping rough for at least a year now."

"I knew it had to be for a good while. I've heard of his socks problem before, and it doesn't happen overnight. Yet he looked so young; he could easily be only fourteen or fifteen."

John shook his head. "No, I think you'll find he was nearer seventeen or eighteen – but I'm afraid I can't be certain of that."

"Does he have any family?"

"Sorry; as I've already said, nobody knows – I mean knew – anything about him. I don't even know his real name. It doesn't do to ask too many questions lest they stop coming to us."

"I see... Well thank you for your help anyway; and I'm sorry to be the bearer of such sad news. Obviously, the police might want to contact you."

"Yes, I realise that. My contact details are on the admission form."

"So I understand. Well once again thank you, and you have my commiserations too."

"Thank you, doctor." John got to his feet and turned sadly away. He then made his way slowly back to the car. The car bleeped and the indicators winked merrily when he pressed the key fob, mocking his dour mood. And when he opened the door, the interior light clearly illuminated the boy's precious sleeping bag lying on the back seat. Just why the death of a boy he hardly knew had hit him so hard he had no idea; but as he climbed into the car, he found that tears were flowing freely down his cheeks. He drew several deep breaths and gradually pulled himself together. He fumbled the key into the lock, and started the engine.

The short drive back to the kitchen seemed to go on forever, and during that eternity he was plagued by disturbing thoughts of sorrow and guilt. Could he have done more to help the poor boy? *Should* he have done more to help him? He prayed the Lord would show his soul the mercy that John had failed to show while he was alive.

When he arrived at Market Square, he was unsurprised to see that Jenny and Anne were shutting down and clearing up. He *was* surprised, however, to see Derek still there lending a hand. Quickly, he parked the car and walked slowly towards them. As he approached, Derek stopped struggling with the tent and walked to meet him.

"How is he?" he asked in a concerned voice.

John closed his eyes for a moment and took a breath. "I'm afraid he passed away without coming round. He...he was much sicker than we ever imagined."

For a second or two Derek said nothing. "Shame," he eventually said, and then added a cryptic, "Cath will be upset to hear it."

"Who's Cath?" Anne asked as she approached them. The van was now safely packed and was only waiting for the folded-down tent.

"Just a lady we both know. I think she was the nearest thing he had to family; for a short while anyway."

"How did he know her?" John asked curiously. "It's just that the police will want to identify him and they'll need to speak to anyone who knew him."

"I'm not sure she'll want to speak to them," Derek replied warily. "She likes to keep herself to herself, if you know what I mean?"

"Please tell us," Anne said touching his arm. "I promise we won't say anything unless she wants us to."

Derek looked from one to the other and then over at Jenny who was now standing beside the open rear doors of the van waiting for the tent. "All right," he conceded at last. "But don't say anything to anyone. I'll ask her to contact you if she has anything she wants to say."

"But who is she," pressed John, unusually eager to garner confidential information.

"Her name's Catherine, she owns that big house off South Cross Lane; the one with the donkeys."

"Mrs Wilmington-Smythe?" Anne exclaimed incredulously. "How on Earth did *she* know him?"

Derek shrugged. "None of my business. I just know she was very fond of him."

John was puzzled. "Derek, if you don't mind me asking, how do *you* know her? She seems a very prickly sort of person for..."

"For the likes of me?" Derek interrupted bitterly.

"No, that's not what I meant. It's just she has a manner that sort of... well... puts people off."

The old man looked at him with eyes that once rheumy and tired, were now bright and defiant. "Maybe so; but I speak as I find and I say she's a better person than any I've met so far."

"But how *did* you meet her?" Anne persisted gently.

Derek stared at her thoughtfully then returned his attention to John. A tense silence ensued. His brow furrowed and he bit his lip as he contemplated revealing something so vitally secret.

CHAPTER TWELVE – *"PRIDE GOES BEFORE DESTRUCTION, A HAUGHTY SPIRIT BEFORE A FALL." (PROVERBS 16:18)*

Derek – The Fourth Prayer

It was exactly one year, and one month before Reverend Winters' soup kitchen anniversary, and Derek Reginald Forsythe was sitting on the grey, knobbly steps of the main entrance to a small but respectable office block in south-east London. And the fact that it was so respectable meant it wouldn't be too long before security came out and moved him on. After all, the sight of a stinking, filthy and emaciated wreck of an old man sitting at the front door was hardly conducive to good business. But the worst of it was, he'd once worked there. But not just worked there, he'd been the most senior manager of a company based in this very building. Once he would have had the power not just to order those security guards around, he'd have had enough power to have them fired. How, he wondered, had it come to this?

It was a stupid question. He knew exactly how, why, and when the spiral down into this particular version of hell had started. Or did he? Was it when he was given that final promotion, the one he'd fought so hard for? Or did it go back further than that? Perhaps back to the day when he'd taken what had at first seemed a dreary but steady job with Jenson Plastics. Was that really only nine years ago? Derek swallowed hard and nodded to himself. Yes, that was when it had started – or at the most, a year before that when the world's financial system had gone into meltdown. He'd been an executive with a well-known investment corporation when the banks had imploded. He'd gone from a high-flyer to the ranks of the unemployed within the space of just forty-eight hours.

At first things hadn't been too bad. Although the mortgage on their large and exclusive, four-bedroom house in the best part of London's commuter belt had been astronomical, he and his wife, Dianna, had had enough put away to keep them going for a good few months – if they were frugal that is. Unfortunately, 'frugal' wasn't a word that Dianna was too familiar with. She'd refused to shop in the "common people's" supermarkets and had still insisted on buying only "quality produce" from "reputable" establishments. And their fifteen-year-old daughter, Charlotte, was no better. The growing strain and dwindling resources had caused fierce arguments that had become more and more acrimonious as the weeks had gone by. And neither did they receive any social security benefits. Although he'd claimed, they had far too many assets to qualify. He still had to sign on every fortnight though. That way, he'd automatically start receiving payments when he'd exhausted his funds.

One day, he'd had enough. Finally, he'd sat both of them down and had shown them the hard facts. It was a lesson in finances that was long overdue for young Charlotte. He'd shown them the sum total of their savings and the sum total of their outgoings. He'd then divided the one by the other to make it clear that within six weeks they'd be defaulting on all their credit cards, but more importantly, on their mortgage. In much less than six months, *he* would not only be unemployed, *they* would be homeless!

Dianna had blanched as the message had finally sunk in. Then at last they'd begun to work together, ticking off the many things they could do without.

The club memberships, Dianna's frequent shopping trips with her friends (along with the accompanying expensive lunches), outings, gym memberships, dinner dates. And they would have to go down to one car. Both BMWs were on finance and would have to go. Fortunately, there was enough equity in them both to part exchange them for a single second hand Ford Focus or the like. He'd also researched the price differences between shops such as Waitrose and M&S, and the likes of Asda and Tesco. He'd then been able to demonstrate that by changing their diet and switching to supermarket own-brands, the weekly shopping bill could be reduced by as much as eighty percent. And that didn't even take into account the many more elite establishments Dianna regularly frequented. By taking all these measures, they'd be able to keep the wolf from the door for an extra six months.

It would also help if Dianna could return to work. She'd blanched again. She had once been a successful personal assistant to the proprietor of a rather high-class publishing house; but she'd given up her career when Charlotte had come along. Derek had neither encouraged nor discouraged that decision; he'd felt that it was hers and hers alone to make. In the end – perhaps because a difficult birth meant that Charlotte would always be an only child – she'd decided to be a stay-at-home mum.

And therein lay the problem with Charlotte; she'd been spoiled beyond measure.

"This is ridiculous!" she'd almost screamed. "Why are you doing this to me? This is like child abuse!"

"Darling, don't exaggerate," Dianna had countered somewhat meekly.

"I am *not* exaggerating. How can I face my friends if I'm a pauper dressed in rags? Oh my God; I won't have any friends after this."

Derek had decided this had gone far enough. "If that's the case, they weren't real friends in the first place!" he'd stated firmly.

"But sweetheart..." Dianna had begun to say, laying a hand on his arm.

"No, Dianna," Derek had interrupted in a commanding voice. "No more pandering to her. Charlotte, you'll just have to put up with it – and worse if we can't find jobs soon."

"This is so unfair!" she'd shrieked. "Why should I have to suffer just because you're a total failure?!" She'd then run up to her bedroom, slamming the door shut so hard it had echoed around the house.

Salvation had come with that fortuitous, but unimpressive job offer at Jenson Plastics. He was to become a mere supervisor in one of their several factories, but at least it covered their now more sensible outgoings.

Of course, Charlotte had been horrified again. "Oh my God," she'd wailed. "Now you're a *factory worker*!"

It had actually been a more satisfying job than he'd expected. There had been problem after problem to deal with. And those problems had meant overtime, and overtime had meant more money. Sometimes, if there had been enough of those problems to handle, there had been enough overtime to almost double his wages.

The reason for it all was simple: Roger Martin. A nice enough man, but an appalling factory manager. He'd had good people-skills but he was young and inexperienced and couldn't organize the proverbial in a brewery. He simply hadn't been up to the job, and only had it in the first place because of some form of nepotism that Derek couldn't quite fathom. Not that Derek had minded, of course. He'd relished the pressure, and his liking for Roger meant that he'd been glad to cover his mistakes. And Roger had always been grateful for his efforts. Eventually though, head office had begun to notice Derek's managerial quality. That was when Roger's attitude had changed. He had now begun to snipe at him, trying to undermine his growing reputation, which was something Derek couldn't allow.

But Derek was a good man; ambitious – even driven – but nonetheless good. So he hadn't retaliated, returning evil for evil; he'd simply stopped covering for the man. Thus, Roger had dug his own grave. Eventually he'd been 'promoted' sideways and his job had been given to Derek; and Derek had dragged the factory kicking and screaming into the twenty-first century. There'd been many complaints from the shop floor but head office didn't care; their only concern was profit; and profit from Derek's factory had risen by twenty percent! The only down side had been Derek's wages.

As a manager, he now drew a salary, which although higher than his previous basic wage, was slightly lower once his overtime had been added into the mix. And of course, any overtime he now worked had become unpaid. Even so, he'd continued to work far more hours than any other manager; and once again, head office had noticed. Another promotion had followed a year later. Once again, he was an executive, and once again Charlotte could hold her head up with the few friends who had remained loyal. But now his ambition had become a creature in its own right, and a destructive one at that.

He'd stayed progressively later at the office; he'd had more and more business dinners, networking and expanding his reputation. And the more he'd had, the more successful he'd become; and the more successful he'd become, the more work he did. He'd begun to believe he was indispensable; only *he* had had the vision and insight to make the company successful; and one day, it would be all his. Although he hadn't realised it, he'd been spinning dangerously out of control. Something had to crack, and eventually, just seven years after starting at Jenson, it did.

He'd become paranoid, certain that his colleagues were jealous and were plotting against him. Then he'd become certain that Dianna was having an affair. He'd even had her followed, which had been a terrible mistake, because it turned out that she was. Then, as his home life had imploded, his work had suffered to; and all those colleagues whom he'd feared were circling like sharks had moved in for the kill. It had all ended in a total, complete and utter, mental breakdown.

He'd been sectioned; so ill that he'd been hospitalised for six months. He had been released to discover that his old life had now gone for good. Jenson had fired him, his wife had left him for her lover, his daughter had disowned him, and his house had been repossessed. There'd been nothing left for him but the streets and the occasional hostel.

And now here he was back outside Jenson Plastics' head office; an alcoholic, filthy and emaciated ruin who was on the point of death after two years of sleeping rough. He put his head in his hands and despaired. Why had God damned him to this living hell, he wondered? But that thought was immediately followed by another. God had not damned him; he had damned himself. True, he'd not been responsible for the circumstances, but only he had been responsible for the way he'd reacted to them.

He was suddenly and acutely aware of all his wrongs, and of all those that he'd hurt. "Oh God, I'm so sorry," he muttered as he began to weep. "Please God, oh please; let me make amends." Something deep inside him seemed to cry out to Heaven.

"Come on mate," a voice said firmly but not unkindly. "You can't stop here."

Derek looked up to see a stern-faced security guard looking down at him.

"Go on old man, off you go. You'll have to find somewhere else to sit and mope."

CHAPTER THIRTEEN –
"BLESSED IS THE MAN WHO ENDURES TEMPTATION..." (JAMES 1:12)

Derek – The Fourth Prayer

I t wasn't a long walk back to the area where Derek had made his home, but in his enervated condition, it took almost an hour. Several times he needed to stop and rest a while. By the time he arrived he was becoming desperate for a drink. His hands were now starting to shake and his nerves were crying out in anguish. Added to that, his breathing was becoming strained and his heartbeat frighteningly irregular. He needed money, and he needed it fast. So he settled himself down outside a row of shops on a well-trodden pedestrian walkway and begged.

He couldn't understand it. Normally he would be sure to find a steady dribble of change tossed into his lap, but nobody seemed to even see him. His plaintive, "Spare some change?" grew louder and more desperate with every few minutes that passed; but it was as if he had become invisible. Nothing, not even a five pence piece came his way. As the afternoon turned to evening and then into night, his withdrawal grew so severe, it was affecting his eyesight. Even with his mind jangling and unable to stay fixed on any thought except alcohol, he retained enough reason to realise it was time to give up. If he didn't make his way to his hideaway soon, he would never be able to find it.

Somehow, he climbed unsteadily to his feet and then managed to stagger the two hundred yards to the alleyway he called home. The alleyway was situated between two shops, and there between all the huge rubbish bins, he'd made a small camp out of cardboard boxes and old newspapers. He also had a large sheet of clear polythene that he could string between the bins to form a kind of tent. The shop workers tolerated his presence, treating him with a form of disgusted sympathy. He just had to make sure to remember when the bins were due for emptying.

Apart from the fact that it overlooked a railway, it was as comfortable a home as he'd had for some time, and one that had kept him alive long past the day he should have succumbed to the elements. And even better, a few feet away an overflow pipe near the top of the building was supplying a constant trickle of water to drink. All in all, it was perfect. Now he crawled into his makeshift camp and curled up ready for the onslaught of agony to come. He just hoped that by the morning he'd be well enough to make another, more successful attempt to glean some money.

In spite of the combined demons of both his past and the alcohol withdrawal tearing at his mind, he somehow made it through the night. Then shaking like an aspen leaf in a breeze, he made his unsteady way back to the spot where he'd begged so unsuccessfully the previous day. Vaguely he remembered offering up a prayer yesterday. No wait, he *had* said a prayer. It had been a good prayer, an honest prayer; surely God would take pity on him because of it. God wouldn't forget him, would he? He decided a reminder would do no harm.

"God," he muttered blearily through his fogged and tormented haze. "Give me some money. I'll die if you don't give me a drink. Please give me a drink." But if God had heard him, the answer was a definite and resounding, "No!"

He begged all day. Out of the hundreds of people who walked past him, he received nothing more than a handful of disgusted looks. By the time he returned to his camp, he was a terrible and pitiful wreck. Just as he had the previous night, he crawled into his plastic and cardboard home and awaited the onslaught. And when it came, it was different to before. Then, he'd felt sure he was going to die, this time he wished that he could. This time when morning came, he was in no fit state to go and beg. He just lay entombed within the cardboard and newspaper, sweating and moaning inaudibly. The flame of his life was flickering, drawing perilously close to being extinguished.

The day passed and darkness fell. He tried to sleep but his heart was beating so fast, it terrified him – but not as much as the strange, shadowy spectres that flashed in front of his eyes. Once he was sure he could see a tiger stalking towards him ready to pounce. He knew however, that the apparitions were nothing more than hallucinations brought on by alcohol withdrawal – the DTs.

Around midnight, he heard strange voices nearby. Two voices in fact, and they grew rapidly louder as their owners drew near. Soon it was clear they were now in the alley. He quietly lifted his cardboard covering just enough to peer out into the darkness. He could just make out two men, and from the way they were staggering, and from the pronounced slurring of their voices, they were obviously very drunk indeed. Derek felt a wave of bitter jealousy sweep over him. What a waste. Why did these two get to drink? To them it was just recreation whereas he *needed* it!

"Are you sure we can cut through here?" one of them asked. At least that's what it sounded like to Derek. The man was so inebriated it was hard to be entirely sure.

"Course I'm sure," the second man replied, slurring even more unintelligibly than his companion. At that moment a train passed along the nearby tracks. "See; I told you. There's a train."

They staggered to the end of the alley where they discovered their error.

The second man swore violently at the first. "And now we've got to go all the way back round!" He cursed some more and the two drunks came back. But just as they were passing Derek's cardboard bed, one of them stopped.

"Wassa matter?" the other man asked.

"I'm gonna...gonna..." There then came the distinct sound of vomiting as the man was violently sick.

"You all right?"

For a few moments the sick drunk was unable to reply. He seemed to be having enough trouble just breathing. "Yeah, I'm okay," he said once he'd pulled himself back together. "I don't want this though." He then flung something towards the bins where Derek was ensconced. Whatever it was, it landed just a couple of feet from his head. The two interlopers then staggered out of the alley and disappeared, presumably headed towards the station. After a few minutes Derek's curiosity got the better of him and he reached out to see exactly what it was that had been thrown.

It was a small parcel, and from its faint aroma, Derek knew exactly what it was. He ripped it open and attacked the large size donner kebab in a famished frenzy of starvation. But as ravenous as he was, his stomach had shrunk so much that he could barely manage to eat half. Carefully, he rewrapped the remains and lay back down to sleep. He hugged his precious windfall to his chest and then closed his eyes; but not before looking to the sky and muttering a heartfelt, "Thank you."

He awoke next morning to face the worst day so far in his enforced and unwelcome detox. Once again, he was unable to leave his bed other than to drink some of the overflowing water. At some point in the afternoon he managed to eat some more of the kebab – now cold and greasy – but that was the extent of his movements until the morning of the day after that. Although still suffering, it did seem that the crisis had passed. By what he judged to be midday, he felt strong enough to make yet another attempt to obtain enough money to end his torment – no matter how temporary that reprieve might be.

And so he made his way to his accustomed spot and settled into the doorway. It seemed he had guessed right about the time. Amongst the shoppers there were a good many people walking around with bags of hot food – some from bakers' shops, but most from the McDonald's just along the walkway. He closed his eyes for a moment and again asked God to supply him with the money for a much-needed drink. He then began his usual litany of, "Any spare change?" It soon became clear that he was still cursed with his recently acquired invisibility. A dark cloud of despair was rising up within him until another strange event occurred.

Two girls, both in their late teens were walking past with McDonald's bags when one of them stopped a few feet away.

"Come on Shaz," her friend called anxiously. "We'll be late."

"Hang on, I just want to check..." She pulled out the burger carton and opened it. "Oh for crying out loud!" she exclaimed. "They've put sauce on it. I distinctly said, 'no sauce'. I'll have to take it back and get it changed."

"Shaz!" her friend wailed incredulously. "We haven't got time. You can't be late again; you're on a written warning already."

"Well I can't eat this..." Her profane description of the offending burger was enough to make a sailor blush. She caught sight of Derek out of the corner of her eye. "There you go, mate," she said handing it to him. "Here's a Big Mac for you. Looks like it's your lucky day." She then ran off to join her friend leaving Derek staring after them open mouthed. He might not be getting a drink, but twice now he'd been provided with some food.

"Thank you," he muttered before demolishing the hamburger. But whether his thanks were directed at the girl or God, even Derek could never remember.

* * *

The next few days were much the same; no money but an occasional lucky break food-wise. Nothing as spectacular as a whole kebab or hamburger, but the odd half a sandwich or a discarded part-portion of chips. Again, cold and greasy but tasty enough when your starving. Then on the night of the fourth day since the hamburger – Friday night – Derek was in his camp when once again he heard people enter the alley. This time there appeared to be three men, and these were most definitely not drunk.

"What you going to do wiv it, Ricky?" one of them asked in an urgent, hushed and youthful voice.

"I'm going to hide it in one of these bins, innit. No one's ever gonna find it there." From their accents Derek was sure the men were black. It struck a note of fear through his body – there were a lot of gangs in this area.

"But suppose the old bill go searching through everything; you know like on the telly?"

"What's the matter wiv you bruv? This ain't CSI."

"Ricky's right, Ash," said a third voice. "Once the bin-men have been, that's it; it's gone forever, like."

Ash just grunted noncommittedly as Ricky made his way over to the bins. Unfortunately, he failed to spot Derek's makeshift home between them. He tripped on it and half-fell, driving his knee painfully into the old man's side. Derek let out a loud, excruciated cry.

"What the...?" Ricky exclaimed in surprise.

In an instant all three of them pounced on him, dragging him out into the shadowy half-light coming in from the street. In the gloom Derek could just make out that there were three youths, probably no more than sixteen or seventeen years old. Although it was too dark to get a good look at their features, it was clear that he'd been wrong. In spite of their accents, only one of them was black. Two of them – the unnamed one and their leader, Ricky – were white.

"It's a dosser!" Ricky exclaimed with fierce joy.

"What are we going to do wiv him bro?" asked the unnamed youth.

"I fink we should have some fun wiv him," Ricky replied malevolently.

"No man," Ash weighed in. Although his dark skin made his features even more indistinguishable than his friends, Derek was sure they were tinged with fear. "Just leave him. We need to get going before there's trouble, innit. Ain't you had enough fun wiv that gay boy?"

"Shut it, Ash," the unnamed one said harshly. "Ricky knows what he's doing."

"Please," Derek said in pathetic and plaintive voice. "Please leave me alone.

But Derek's plea seemed to be the spark that ignited the explosion. With a vicious cry, Ricky started kicking the old man and the anonymous youth swiftly joined in. Ash walked away towards the street, ostensibly to keep a look out for any witnesses. Again and again they kicked him with what should have been life-threatening force. Somehow though, perhaps because the darkness spoiled their aim, the most powerful of the kicks were scuffed. And although Derek was badly winded and his body was badly bruised, his head remained untouched throughout the whole attack.

When finally the ordeal ended, Derek played dead, letting himself go as limp as he could. Ricky bent down and pulled him up by the front of his tatty jacket. Derek let his head flop back and held his breath. For a few moments the young thug peered at him closely, trying to penetrate the gloom. Then with a triumphant snort, he threw Derek's lifeless form back onto the ground.

"Is he still breathing?" Ricky's accomplice asked breathlessly.

"No, he's as dead as that queer-boy, innit."

"Let's get out of here then. Dump the wallet and let's go."

Ricky stared thoughtfully down at Derek's body. "Here bruv, I just had a thought." The feral little murderer then knelt down beside the stricken old man and slipped something into his coat pocket. "There; they'll find the old dosser and they'll find the wallet in his pocket. They'll think he did the poofter in, won't they."

"Man, that's genius; and I ain't even lyin' though."

"Tell me, bruv; tell me. Now let's go."

The murderous thugs ran off, collecting their lookout, Ash, on the way.

Derek lay still for what seemed an eternity, terrified that his tormentors would return. Eventually, almost an hour later, he crawled stiffly and painfully back to his cardboard den and fell into a deep sleep.

He awoke next morning and examined himself. He was surprised to discover just how little damage he'd actually suffered. Although he was in a lot of pain – particularly in his left shoulder – nothing seemed to be broken. Derek let out an ironic snort. He was either lucky to be so unscathed or unlucky to have been attacked in the first place.

His biggest surprise came when he pulled the wallet from his pocket. It was a small, expensive-looking affair. It was made of pig skin and was so light a brown as to almost pink. Derek flipped it open and examined it closely. Stamped on the left side was a bright red heart while on the right there were two names, deeply embossed in gold. It seemed pretty clear that it had belonged to the gay man the three thugs had apparently murdered.

At first he thought the wallet was empty, but for some unfathomable reason the thieves had left something behind. Puzzled, Derek pulled it out and examined it. It was a train ticket. After thoroughly searching the wallet to see if there was anything else the muggers had missed, he put the ticket back and closed the wallet.

What was he to do? By all rights he should take it to the police, but the thought of that filled him with trepidation. His experience with the boys in blue over the past two years had not been good. And anyway, although he was sorry that the man was dead, he was part of a society that Derek no longer belonged to. It was nothing to do with him. But he would not do as Ricky had been about to do last night; he would not throw it into one of the bins. He decided to leave it lying at the end of the alley and let luck take its course. If it was meant to be found, it would be. But unlike his stupid erstwhile murderer, he would wipe his finger prints away first – just in case.

He picked up a piece of newspaper to hold it by and began to vigorously wipe it on his trousers. First, he did the outside and then started on the inside. As he did, he dislodged the train ticket, sending it fluttering to the ground. He tutted to himself and picked it up again. It was when he was about to return it to the wallet that he stopped dead and stared at the gold, embossed inscription. Although he obviously now needed reading glasses, the writing was large enough for him to read. Apparently, the wallet had been given to the murdered man by his male lover, and in a beautifully swooping script it read:

Joshua Loves Dietrich

Sometime in the past he'd discovered that Joshua was the Hebrew version of Jesus, but he also knew that Dietrich was the German version of Derek. He swallowed hard and examined the ticket more closely. The writing was too small to read clearly, but by holding it at arm's length and squinting, he could just make out enough to make a guess at what it said.

It appeared to be an open, anytime ticket from here to somewhere he couldn't quite decipher. Was the inscription a sign that he should use the ticket and leave London? He frowned and tried to focus even harder. He moved the ticket closer and then back to arm's length again and again. As far as he could make out, the ticket would take him from Woolwich Arsenal to somewhere that seemed to be called Redwood or Renwood; or maybe even, Rewford.

CHAPTER FOURTEEN –

"THOSE WHO HAVE REVERENCE FOR THE LORD WILL LEARN FROM HIM THE PATH THEY SHOULD FOLLOW." (PSALM 25:12)

Derek – The Fourth Prayer

D erek stood looking at the train, his body frozen by indecision. It had been one thing to travel to Kings Cross from Woolwich – after all, he knew London well – but to take such a huge leap into the unknown was altogether different. It turned out that he'd guessed right about the destination, but he didn't even know where Rewford was! And was he fit enough to make the transition – or even the journey, come to that?

It was now Monday the twenty-second of October – almost a month since he'd found the ticket, a month during which he had procrastinated no end. He had wavered to the point where it seemed certain he was going to stay in Woolwich. Throughout those weeks, whether it was from his own determination or by sheer bad luck, he had managed to stay sober. He had also seen the headlines of a newspaper. It turned out that Dietrich had not been killed after all. The Homophobic attack had been captured on CCTV and the three thugs had been quickly arrested. They were now looking at a very harsh sentence indeed. His profound relief had finally provided him with the impetus he needed to go. But now that he was standing on this platform, his doubts had returned with a vengeance. His hesitation was about to overcome his resolve when he was brought back to Earth by a female voice at his side.

She was a young woman, in her early twenties with shoulder length brown hair. Her gently smiling face was pleasant and attractive, despite her having applied only the minimum of makeup. She was wearing a knee length grey coat, and a long, thick green scarf wrapped loosely around her neck. Over her shoulder was slung a huge, long-strapped handbag. Derek could not believe she was talking to him. Surely he was mistaken.

"I said hello," she repeated, her smile growing broader.

"Erm... hello," replied Derek warily.

"I'm sorry to bother you," she said in a voice brimming with an odd mixture of confidence and trepidation. "But I was standing over there with my friend..." She gestured along the platform to where another woman was standing watching them. "...and I felt moved to come over and speak to you."

"Erm... Why?" Derek's confusion was profound and obvious.

"Oh, it happens like that sometimes. Please don't be offended but I wanted to give you this." She reached into her voluminous bag and pulled out a fair-sized Tupperware box that obviously contained her packed lunch.

Derek was even more confused. "But why would you want to do that? Won't you need it?" In spite of his words, his hand was already reaching for the proffered box.

"Oh, it's all right; I can share Claire's; she's packed far too much for the journey anyway.

"Thank you," Derek breathed gratefully, the box now firmly in his possession. "But you still haven't told me why."

The girl's smile softened and a look of deep compassion filled her eyes. "Because I'm a Christian, and when the Lord gives me a nudge, I try to obey him. And he definitely just gave me a nudge."

"I see," said Derek, clearly having no idea what she meant.

The girl chuckled; a musical sound that was infectious enough to make Derek's lips twitch into a faint grin. "My name's Rachael," she said holding out her hand.

Automatically, Derek reached out to take it, but then he suddenly pulled away in horror. His hands were hideously filthy and all kinds of disgusting muck and grime were lodged under his fingernails. In contrast, Rachael's hands were pristine, her nails clean and neatly manicured.

But she clearly had no qualms, for she took hold of his hand anyway and then held it firmly between *both* of hers. "So what's yours?" she asked gently.

Derek swallowed hard. This was getting unsettlingly surreal. "It's Derek," he said at last.

"Well Derek, it's lovely to meet you."

Derek's mouth opened and closed but his confusion had left him tongue-tied.

"Tell me Derek, do you believe in God?" she asked, peering deep into his eyes.

Instantly, Derek's defences went up, shutting out the friendship the girl appeared to be offering. "No!" he replied firmly, just as he had when he'd still been human.

"Really?" Rachael asked dubiously.

Derek started to reply, but then his prayer on the steps outside Jenson's offices flashed into his mind; and along with that came the memories of a kebab and a Big Mac, along with all the other things he'd found to eat recently. And wasn't his enforced detox also an answer to that prayer? True, he'd repeatedly asked for a drink and hadn't got one, but wasn't that an answer in itself? And if he didn't believe in God, why was he standing on this platform in the first place.

He swallowed. "I suppose I do," he conceded lamely.

The girl nodded understandingly. "Can I give you something else?" she asked in a voice that was so plaintive, he had no option but to grunt an affirmative.

"Thank you," she replied with a huge smile of gratitude. She let go of his hand and again reached into her bag. She pulled out a kind of plastic wallet, took something from it, and then handed it to Derek.

It was a small plastic rectangle about half the size of a credit card. Three white crosses were standing on a hill while above it all were four lines of writing. He held it out at arm's length and squinted at it, but even then, the letters were very small and the handwritten style of the script made it impossible for him to read.

"It's very nice," he said flashing her a stained-toothed smile. "Thank you."

"Can you read what it says?"

"Not without my reading glasses, but I'm sure it's lovely."

Amazingly, she put a hand on his shoulder. "Do you *have* any reading glasses?" she asked softly.

"Erm...well... Erm..." Why did he feel so ashamed?

"It's all right," she said rescuing him from his embarrassment. "I can tell you what it says. It's called the sinner's prayer. It's a prayer asking Jesus into your life and then giving your life to him in return. But it's a prayer you should only say if it's from the heart. But if you say it, and you mean it, your life will never be the same again."

Derek let out a scornful laugh. "Look at me girl, do you seriously believe he could change *my* life?"

"Derek," she scolded gently, actually putting her arm around his shoulders. "Nobody's a lost cause in Jesus' eyes – especially you."

He stared blindly at the card, his heart a turmoil of emotions. "Are you sure?" he whispered.

Somehow, Rachael heard him even above the noise of the station. "Of course I'm sure; he changed *my* life which was a miracle in itself, believe me."

"But I don't know anything about Jesus – except maybe Christmas and a couple of things I learned at school."

"Ah, but he knows everything about you."

Derek sighed. "Which is why there's no hope for me."

"Which is why he died for you. There's no hope for any of us without him. But he gave his life on the cross for us all. It doesn't matter what we might have done in the past, his sacrifice washes away all sin from those who turn to him."

Derek looked into her eyes. Nobody had stood so close to him for years. Her head was almost touching his and there was not a trace of revulsion on her face. "Really?" he asked, his voice choked with emotion.

"Really."

"Can... will..."

"Would you like me to say the prayer with you?"

Derek nodded, unable to speak his reply. He had no problem repeating after Rachael though, and she clearly knew the prayer by heart. So, with tears flowing freely down his cheeks, he prayed to Jesus.

"Dear Lord Jesus; thank you for dying on the cross for my sins. Please forgive me. I believe you rose again from the dead. Come into my life; I receive you as my Lord and saviour. Help me to live the rest of my life for you. In the name of Jesus I pray. Amen."

He had no idea why, but for a few moments after, he wept like a baby. Rachael kept her arm around him and just let him cry. But then the whistle blew and it was time for her to join her friend.

"Goodbye, Derek," she said quietly. "God bless." She then squeezed his shoulders and hurried away.

"Goodbye," he whispered, wiping away his tears. Then, with his mind finally decided, he boarded the train.

CHAPTER FIFTEEN – *"IT IS GOD WHO CLOTHES THE WILD GRASS... WON'T HE BE ALL THE MORE SURE TO CLOTHE YOU?" (MATTHEW 6:30)*

Derek – The Fourth Prayer

Three weeks after arriving in Rewford, Derek knew he was coming to the end. Although he was getting some reward from his begging, it was only a fraction of what he used to get in Woolwich – at least before the Lord had forced him to stop drinking. And he was now in no doubt that his 'drying out' had been God's work. But just why he'd sent him to Rewford, Derek couldn't fathom. Still, he wouldn't have lasted all that much longer down south, and at least Rewford was a nicer place to die. And of course, there was the nightly hot meal at the reverend's kitchen. It wasn't enough to keep him alive for long – not in his parlous state of health – but it was more than he'd been eating for several months before his move. Most of his calories had come from strong cider and lager before his detox. Despite his impending death, however, Derek Reginald Forsythe was at peace with himself. Since asking Jesus into his life, his personal demons had withdrawn, allowing him to sleep easier. They hadn't gone away entirely of course, and they occasionally launched another attack, but he now had a friend to help fight them off. And the more he relied on that friend, the weaker the old anger and bitterness became. And there were two things he possessed that always reminded him both of his promise and the kind girl who'd shown him the way: the card and her lunchbox.

On the morning of Tuesday, the 13th – at least he thought that was the date but it was easy to lose track – he awoke after another unseasonably warm night. Just as well for a couple of weeks ago it had got pretty close to freezing in the early hours. Much more of that and he certainly would have gone to meet his maker. He smiled to himself; that was no longer a prospect that held any fear. And there had been precious little rain, which was another thing to be thankful for.

Unlike his old haunt, he had no real place to lay his head. Although he had found a nice, secluded recess in an alley behind a charity shop, he'd been unable to source any cardboard or plastic sheet. Rewford was a much cleaner and tidier place than southeast London. So although it was picturesque, it made it much harder for the likes of him. All he'd managed to find for his comfort were several old newspapers that he'd liberated from the waste bins which were strategically scattered around town.

He tried to sit up and couldn't help letting out a sharp cry of pain. The joints in his thin, wasted limbs had seized, and when he tried to move them, it felt like they were filled with sharp sand. He took several deep breaths and then tried again; but this time with a great deal more care. Slowly his arms and legs moved more freely and the pain in them eased. After several more minutes he was able to stand.

"Thank you, Jesus," he muttered with a genuine smile. With a start he realised that it was late. He'd slept much longer than usual which he put down to the warmish weather and his newly found peace of mind. He left the alley and looked up and down the road. There was a shoe shop across the way, and since there was a man putting out the racks of shoes,

Derek guessed it must be about nine o'clock. He stood for a few moments deciding which way to go. Left or right? Did it make any difference which way he went? In the end he turned right, if only to stand and stare in the charity shop.

It was a silly thing to do and he knew it. What was the point of torturing himself so? But every morning since he'd first seen the shop, he'd found himself standing there, gazing longingly at the coat in the window. Twenty pounds they wanted for it. A high price in most charity shops he'd seen in Woolwich, but a bargain with this particular charity. And what made it even more of a snip – a giveaway in fact – was the make of the coat.

He'd had one just like it many years ago; except his had been red instead of bright blue. He'd bought it for an alpine skiing holiday and what a wonderful choice it had been. It was waterproof, breathable, and warm beyond belief. But then again, with a staggering price tag of eight hundred pounds, it ought to be. And here was one that looked brand new for just twenty!

He sighed heavily. Even at that price it might just as well have been a million. He caught sight of the woman in the shop. Sometimes there were two of them but this morning she was on her own. She'd just picked up a box of something and was headed through a concealed door that led to the stockroom – or whatever it was they had. After a minute or so she still hadn't returned. An idea flashed into his mind but it was an idea so abhorrent, so against the grain of his nature – no matter how far he'd fallen – that it left him breathless and horrified. He pushed the thought out of his head and forced himself to walk away. Quite how he found himself inside the shop he had no idea. That was what he told himself, anyway.

"I'll be out in a minute," the woman called when she heard the bell above the door. "Just give me a shout if you need any help." Oh, how trusting they were in this town.

Derek tucked his lunchbox under his arm, went over to the coat, and reached out his hands. His chest pounded and the blood sang in his ears. For a second, he hesitated; then he snatched the coat from its hanging and rushed out of the shop.

He didn't run away – that would only draw attention to himself – but he walked as fast as his weak and enervated body would allow. He headed for another secluded alley; one he'd tried as a sleeping place but had discounted because it was overlooked. The five minutes it took to reach it stretched on and on as though made of elastic. Eventually though, he stood pressed safely against a wall, clutching his swag, and hidden from the world outside.

Once his breathing was under control, he made to pull off the ticket but then hesitated. He didn't even know if it was his size. He might have just committed the crime for no reason at all. Sweating profusely, he pulled off his own tattered and crumpled jacket and slipped into the wondrous garment.

So strong was the feeling of opulent luxury, he almost fainted. And when he realised that it fitted – albeit one size too big – he almost started to cry. But then a thought hit him. What had he done? Would Jesus be smiling on him after committing theft? Would he still love him after such a wanton act?

He cursed himself for being so ridiculous. Of course Jesus would understand. Obviously, he was *meant* to steal it; why else would it be there? Despite his protestations however, he knew that he'd been wrong.

But whatever the rights or wrongs, it was done now. The coat was his, and his it would remain. He tried the hood and smiled. He could only imagine how much easier he would sleep tonight. He put his hands in the side pockets and sighed. The soft, fluffy material was almost too wonderful to bear, and to his delight, they had no holes in them. There were two inside pockets to try, although one was hidden – a safe place for valuables when out skiing on the piste. He tried the first and that was also fine. He put his hand into the secret pocket and his brow furrowed. There was something in there that felt like a...

It was a wallet that had obviously been overlooked by the previous owner and the women in the charity shop. He stared at it blankly, his mind flying back to the pigskin wallet that had contained the train ticket. This one however, held far more than that. With trembling hands, he pulled out the notes and began to count them. There were ten twenty-pound notes – two hundred pounds. *Two hundred pounds!* More money than had passed through his hands all year. Slowly, the shock faded and he began to breathe again. Quickly, he stuffed the notes back into the wallet and returned it to the hidden pocket. That was it then; if God had meant him to have the train ticket then surely this was a sign that the coat and its contents were meant to be his too. But what now? Suppose he was seen with the coat? He would surely stick out like a sore thumb, and explaining the money would be impossible. There was only one thing for it; he had to leave Rewford right away.

He picked up his old jacket, checked all its pockets, then rolled it up and threw it into a corner. He wouldn't need that piece of garbage anymore. Then he turned and left the alley and started off in the direction of the station. He'd gone only twenty paces before he turned around and went straight back. He pulled out the wallet and looked at it again. There was a name and address printed on a little card within a clear plastic window. Shouldn't he return it to its rightful owner money and all? Surely that's what Jesus would do. And then another thought struck him. A lovely, deliciously exciting and audacious thought. Again, his hands trembled as he touched the precious twenties; but this time he pulled out only one. He put it into one of the side pockets and then once again secreted the wallet.

This time the woman was in the shop, standing behind the counter. She was busy totting something up on a large calculator when he walked in.

"Good morning," she said pleasantly, lifting her head and smiling. The smile froze on her lips when she saw the coat. She looked over to where it had hung in the window and blanched. Derek breathed a sigh of relief. If she hadn't noticed it was missing, then there was no hue and cry over the theft.

"Good morning," he replied, trying to sound nonchalant. "I hope you can forgive my audacity, but you were busy out back, and I really wanted this coat. Unfortunately, though, I didn't have the money on me. I'm afraid I took it with me so no one else could buy it."

"That's not the way it's done," the woman replied haughtily. Her cheeks were burning red with suppressed anger.

"Yes I know, I'm very sorry; I just wasn't thinking. Anyway, I've got the money now so here you go, twenty pounds." He held out the note and smiled what he hoped was a winning smile. From her reaction however, it was clear it was more of a revolting grimace.

"It's highly irregular," she sniffed, gingerly taking the money between her thumb and forefinger.

"As I say, I'm very sorry. I'll be sure to do things properly next time."

From the way the woman recoiled, it was clear that the thought of this bearded, dirty, hollow-cheeked little troll re-entering her shop was almost too horrifying to bear. So with a polite, "good day," Derek made his exit and returned to the alley.

This time he leant against the wall and laughed. A huge weight had been lifted from his shoulders and he realised that that weight had been guilt. And now he was free of it. Well almost. He took out the wallet and peered at the address. It was no good; the writing was far too small. In a flash of inspiration, he slid the card out from behind the clear plastic and then put the wallet away. He strode confidently back into the street and searched the passers-by for a kindly looking face. In the end he plumped for a young man with smiling eyes and a silly blue and red bobble hat.

"Excuse me," he said as affably as he could. "I need to get to this address but unfortunately I've left my reading glasses at home."

The young man eyed him warily but then grinned. "I know what you mean. I was always losing my glasses but I wear contacts now. Solved the problem completely." He took the card and looked at it closely. "Yes, I know where this is."

"Can you tell me what it says?"

"Of course I can. It says: Major Charles Smythe, Sanctuary House, South Cross Lane, Rewford."

"Thank you very much, young man. I don't suppose you could give me directions, could you?"

The young man smiled again. "Of course I can.

CHAPTER SIXTEEN – *"AS SURELY AS THE LORD LIVES, YOU ARE AN HONEST MAN..."* *(1 SAMUEL 29:6)*

Derek – The Fourth Prayer

S anctuary house was located a short walk from the centre of town in an area that seemed strangely lonely and devoid of civilization. It was an odd-looking place. Derek had never seen such a strange mixture of opulence and drab austerity. A high, well-trimmed hedge surrounded it; protecting its privacy and guarding it as surely as the outer walls defended a castle. Indeed, he half expected there to be a moat and a drawbridge, but instead there was an open, farm-style gate – a large and incongruous chink in the stronghold's defenses. He stood by the gate and surveyed the building and courtyard.

There was no garden as such; just a large, tarmacked yard. The building itself was huge; far bigger than the four-bedroomed house that Derek had once owned. On the ground floor, six large sash windows glared at him with dour disapproval, three each side of the front entrance. Three wide steps led up to a porch that although small, still made room for two supporting columns. But far from being grand or pretentious, these columns were square and fashioned from a drab grey stone. The front door seemed to be made of a dark and forbidding studded oak. On the floor above there were six more of the sash windows, and another was positioned above them between the steeply sloping, steeple-like eaves. It should all have been grand, but every square inch of the walls was covered in a pebble dashing that belonged more on a council estate than on a splendid house such as this. Beside the house was parked a green Land Rover Defender; old but from the look of it, well cared for. The overall impression of the place was almost enough to make him turn tail and run. Yet somehow, the lunchbox under his arm was a reassuring reminder of just why he was here. He took out the wallet, steeled himself and walked through the gate.

There was no doorbell, just a heavy knocker cast into the shape of a threatening, snarling lion. Just one more thing to let any visitors know they were unwelcome. He swallowed hard and gave the door three hard knocks. The booming sound echoed throughout the house, shaking his nerves and bringing his anxiety to a climax. He half expected the door to creak slowly open, and a gaunt, cadaverous-looking butler to appear at the entrance. But instead, the door almost flew open, and rather than the anticipated spectre from a horror movie, it was just an ordinary, flesh and blood woman standing before him. But she towered over him and was such a woman as to strike fear into him, nonetheless.

She was older than Derek, in her late sixties or early seventies, yet in some ways she appeared younger than him. She had long grey hair that she wore in a tightly pulled back ponytail. Her clothes seemed to match the severity of the house. She was wearing a calf-length, grey tweed skirt, and a thick, cream-coloured Arran sweater. For a fraction of a heartbeat her demeanour radiated stern impatience, but then her eyes widened and she let out a surprised, "Well I never!"

"Oh hello," Derek said quickly. "I'm sorry to bother you but I'm looking for Major Smythe; is he here by any chance?"

The woman stared at him for a moment and seemed somewhat perplexed; but then in an instant, her stern expression returned. "Afraid you're a bit late," she said in clipped disparaging tone. "My husband passed away several months ago."

"Oh... erm..."

"Well don't just stand there umming and aah-ing man; what did you want with him?"

"Oh... erm... Are you his wife?"

"I think I made that clear when I said that my *husband* passed away several months ago."

Derek was now getting red-faced and flustered. The urge to turn and run away was overwhelming. "Oh, yes; of course you did."

"Well, spit it out man; I haven't got all day."

"Right... of course... Well I bought this coat at the charity shop in town... and..."

"For goodness sake man; what's the matter with you? I can see it was the Major's coat; I'm not an imbecile. What about it?"

Derek swallowed hard. This was ridiculous. Why did he find this woman so intimidating? He would stand up to her; he would be firm and strong. He may be shorter and more fragile, he may be filthy and decrepit, but he was just as much a human being – and he was on a mission!

"I found this in one of its pockets," he said in a timid voice as he meekly held out the wallet.

The woman raised a puzzled eyebrow. Slowly she reached out and took the wallet. She looked at it for a moment then returned her gaze to Derek. It was a hard look; a look so searching and stern that he actually flinched. She scrutinised him closely. His emaciated, grime-smeared face, his unkempt beard and filthy hair. She looked from one of his dirt ingrained hands to the other and then into his eyes.

"Very kind of you," she said at last. Her face suddenly hardened. "Afraid there'll be no reward though," she added in her brusque and clipped tone.

Derek smiled. "No problem; I didn't expect one. It just seemed only right to bring it back. I found the address on the inside."

The woman opened the wallet and then blinked with surprise. She pulled out the money and began to count it.

"It's all there," Derek said hurriedly, then hung his head. "Well, almost all of it."

She stopped counting and glowered at him. "Almost?"

Derek's embarrassment and shame were overpowering. Never had he felt so guilty in his life. It seemed that her daunting glare was seeing right into his very soul. "I'm afraid I borrowed twenty pounds to buy the coat. I *will* pay it back though," he added in a rush.

The woman finished counting the money then studied his face thoughtfully. "Twenty pounds, eh?

"Yes; but as I said, I'll pay it back."

The woman snorted sceptically. Again, she looked him up and down before giving a sharp nod. "Very well; pay me back now."

Derek was aghast. This was not the response he'd expected. Why was this woman repaying his honesty with such ungrateful hostility?

"Erm...I...erm..."

"Stop stammering man and pay up."

"I... I can't yet."

"Yes you can. There's a hundred and eighty pounds left in the wallet; add in the twenty you stole and it makes two hundred."

"I didn't steal..."

"Now since the usual finder's fee is ten percent, I owe you twenty pounds. So let me see, since I now have a hundred and eighty..." She suddenly grinned. "That's your debt cleared, paid in full."

Derek was stunned, unable to comprehend what she was saying.

"Good grief man, what's the matter with you? You're standing there gulping like a goldfish."

"I... erm..."

"You must stop stammering like that; it makes you sound like a village idiot. Tell me your name man, and don't stammer it, say it."

"It's...it's Derek, Mrs Smythe."

"That's *Wilmington*-Smythe to you. Tell me Derek, do you like donkeys?"

"Sorry?"

"Donkeys man; you know, long ears, Eeyore, they like carrots. Donkeys!"

"Erm... I've never met one."

"What? You never had a donkey ride when you were a boy?"

Derek shook his head mutely.

"Hmm... Terrible. Still, we can't all be privileged enough to have a holiday at the seaside."

"My daughter had a pony though," he countered hurriedly.

Mrs Wilmington-Smythe's eyebrows shot up. "Really?" she asked incredulously.

"Really." Derek replied feeling a faint flush of indignation. He might be a malodourous vagrant now, but how dare she make assumptions about his past.

"And did she appreciate the privilege?"

"Of course she..." Derek paused. Charlotte had not stopped demanding a pony for months, but when she finally got one for her twelfth birthday, the novelty had quickly worn off. "Perhaps not as much as she should have," he said more honestly.

"But did she look after it? Did she feed it, groom it and the like?"

"For a while. To be honest, my wife and I ended up doing most of it. You know what little girls are like."

"If you let them be like it. Spare the rod and all that." Again, she gave him a searching look. "Times change though, don't they Derek?"

Derek bit his lip. What was it about this odd woman that intimidated him so? But in spite of his apprehension, there was something about her he liked. "Yes, Mrs Smythe, they do," he replied quietly.

"*Wilmington*-Smythe!" she snapped. Suddenly, she stepped out of the door and shut it behind her. "Come along, man," she said pushing past him. "And don't dawdle."

She hurried down the steps and turned left towards where Derek knew the Land Rover was parked. Derek watched her open mouthed. He had done his job. He had returned the wallet, now all he wanted to do was leave. This odd woman was far too eccentric for comfort.

Mrs Wilmington-Smythe reached the corner of the house, spun around, and put her hands on her hips.

"What are you waiting for? With me man; and be quick about it."

There was nothing else to do but comply. As soon as he started moving towards her, she gave a grunt of satisfaction and disappeared around the corner. By the time he also rounded the corner, he found her standing in front of the Land Rover and leaning on a gate identical to the one at the front of the house. To his surprise, she was calling out what sounded like, "chew, chew, chew," in a loud, high pitched voice.

When he joined her at the gate, she glanced at him with a strange twinkle in her eye. "Come on, come and meet them." She opened the gate and ushered him through. She followed and shut the gate behind them.

Derek gasped. He had expected to be standing in a good sized, paved back garden with a few large flower pots or at best, a tiny patch of lawn. Instead he was confronted by what could only be described as a grassy field – and a big one at that. He tried to picture how such a place could exist so near to the centre of town, but his mind wasn't that agile. It was bounded on his left by a high fence not far beyond that corner of the house; but to his right, the fence was at least two hundred yards away and probably even further than that to the front of him. In the distance he could just make out the nearest houses of

Rewford town. Along the fence to his left, about twenty yards from the house, was what appeared to be a rough, open stable. And from it, two small donkeys were walking lazily towards them. It didn't take long for them to arrive. They went straight up to their owner and nuzzled her, one of them quite forcefully.

"Stop it, Randy," she said firmly. "It's not dinner time and you know it."

She turned to Derek. "He's very impatient and demanding – just like all men. Here, stroke them."

Slowly, so as not to startle them, he reached out his hand and stroked the neck of the nearest one. The creature looked at him and then nudged his arm pit. Derek chuckled and tickled it under its chin.

"That's Peg. I think she likes you."

Derek felt a lump in his throat. The donkey had no concerns about the way he looked or smelled. It liked him all the same. "She's lovely."

"She is; whereas as this one…" She took hold of Randy's nose and roughly pulled it from side to side. "…is a damned nuisance!" Randy responded by pulling his nose away and pushing forward, almost knocking the woman off her feet. Mrs Wilmington-Smythe burst out laughing. "You see? A damned nuisance."

Derek grinned, "He loves you though," he said admiringly.

"He does." She suddenly became serious again. "You say you used to see to your daughter's pony?"

Derek's face fell. He wished he hadn't mentioned it; the memories were far too painful. "I did," he responded a little sullenly.

"Groom it?"

"Yes."

"Hmm. Got anywhere to sleep?"

Derek mutely shook his head.

She treated him to another of her searching stares. "Right then Derek," she said in her brisk, matter-of-fact manner. "You're obviously honest – the wallet is proof of that – so here's my proposal. You can sleep in the stable over there. It's nothing much, but I'm sure a roof and some straw is better than some of the places you've dossed."

Derek nodded.

"Right. I'll expect something in return though. I'll want Randy and Peg groomed regularly. Maybe you can help feed them too."

"I... I don't know what to say."

"Say thank you once and once only. Any more than once is embarrassing and rude."

"Thank you, Mrs Wilmington-Smythe."

"Right. But remember, you *don't* live here; I'm just allowing you to sleep here at night. Once you've seen to the donkeys in the morning – every morning – I want you gone. Clear?"

Derek couldn't help grinning. "Clear!" he said, snapping to attention. He immediately regretted his cheek; she was likely to throw him off her property for good. He needn't have worried though.

"Good man," she said with a nod of approval. "And we'll drop the Wilmington–Smythe business. The name's Catherine. If we get along, I might let you call me Cath. Come on then, stop dawdling; I'll show you your billet."

CHAPTER SEVENTEEN –

"GOD HAS TOLD HIS PEOPLE, 'HERE IS A PLACE OF REST; LET THE WEARY REST HERE.'" (ISAIAH 28:12)

Derek – The Fourth Prayer

For the first time in two years, Derek awoke fully rested and comfortable. He stretched out luxuriously and then cautiously sat up. Apart from a sharp twinge here and there, he was remarkably pain free and limber. True, he still felt sick and weak, but far less so than of late. He'd made a comfortable bed of straw and Catherine had given him an old and tattered blanket which although covered in stains, was actually very clean and recently washed. Despite its worn and frayed condition, it was also thick, warm, and surprisingly soft.

For the most part, the stable was completely open at the front; but at both ends there was a few feet of wooden frontage which provided at least some protection from the elements. What with that along with all the straw and the blanket, he'd even been warm enough to remove his precious coat. He'd carefully folded it up and had used it as a more than acceptable pillow.

Immediately after showing him the stable – his billet, as she called it – Catherine had almost thrown him off her property. She'd escorted him all the way to the open front gate, but then had uttered a sharp command of, "Stop! Wait here." She'd then hurried back to the house and in through the front door, almost slamming it shut behind her. He'd stood waiting for a good five minutes before she'd returned. She'd marched up to him and had slapped something into his hand.

"There," she'd said coldly. "I assume you'll be visiting Reverend Winters' food van tonight, and I can't have you blundering around in the dark when you come back. I *don't* want to be woken up!" The object was a small windup LED torch. "And since you don't look as though you'll survive until then, you'd better have these – after all, I want my torch back."

She'd handed him a small paper bag which had contained half-a-dozen chocolate biscuits. Not much, but they had indeed kept him going until his hot meal. Although he had been given two pounds fifty from passers-by during the day, he'd spent only eighty pence of it on a can of drink. With his mouth watering and his stomach rumbling, he'd stubbornly resisted all the snacks and chocolate on offer in the newsagent shop. For some reason he felt the need to start saving, but saving up for what he had no idea.

He stretched again and looked around the stable. He smiled to himself. Randy and Peg were standing close by, seemingly unwilling to go out into the field until their new companion was awake. In fact, Peg had taken to him so much, he'd half expected her to lay down next to him. It was clear however, that just like Charlotte's pony, donkeys preferred to sleep standing up.

"Good morning Randy, good morning Peg."

Randy paid him no heed, but Peg looked at him and snorted a cheery greeting. Randy then trotted out of the stable and after another friendly snort, Peg followed on behind.

"Bye then," he chuckled. "See you later." As he pulled his coat out from behind him, his eyes fell on his lunchbox. What a change of direction his life had taken recently; and on reflection, he knew exactly when that change had begun. It had all started on the steps outside his old offices when at his lowest of lows, he'd prayed. Not that he'd appreciated the change at first. Those initial few weeks had been hard – very hard. And it did seem that God had cursed rather than blessed him. Although most of his memories were clouded by a haze of alcohol abuse, he clearly remembered that heartfelt prayer outside Jenson's. And contrary to how it had seemed, from that very moment, slowly but surely, God *had* been blessing him. And then he'd given his new life to Jesus.

"Thank you, Lord," he breathed. "Thank you, Jesus." Suddenly he frowned. Who exactly *was* Jesus? There were some half-forgotten bible stories about him, and he knew that Christmas had something to do with his being born in a stable. And of course, he usually got a mention at Easter; but other than that, he drew a blank. Yet he knew Jesus was there because he could feel him. From the moment he'd said the sinner's prayer with Rachael at Kings Cross he'd known. But what did it mean? What was he supposed to *do* about it?

He closed his eyes. "Jesus," he whispered. "Show me what you want. I've got nothing to give you, but whatever you want from me, it's yours."

He waited; he listened; he waited some more. But there was nothing; no voice, no flash of inspiration, nothing. Eventually he sighed and opened his eyes again. He could tell that Jesus was still there, and he hadn't left him, but Derek was none the wiser about just who he was. He needed to find out.

But first he had a job to do. He climbed to his feet and put his coat on. As he went to do it up, he looked down and saw his own clothes. The contrast between the pristine, outrageously luxurious coat and his old disgustingly filthy, reeking rags struck him like physical blow. Somehow, he needed to rectify the situation, but in the meantime, there were more important things to consider. He finished zipping up the coat and moved to a shelf on the back wall of the stable. From there he picked up two coarse brushes and then turned and walked out into the field.

The two Donkeys were now a good way off now, standing close to the far fence and having a good munch of grass.

"Peg! Randy!" he called loudly. Peg lifted her head slightly and glanced his way but then immediately went back to her grazing. Randy once again ignored him completely. "Come on you two," he shouted even louder. "Come over here for a good brushing." This time even Peg snubbed him. Suddenly, Derek had a flash of inspiration.

"Chew, chew, chew!" he shouted, emulating Catherine's voice as best he could. Both donkeys lifted their heads and looked at him. "Chew, chew, chew!" he repeated. He laughed loudly as the pair of them came trotting happily towards him.

"Right then, which one of you is first." With a brush in each hand he looked from one expectant face to the other. In the end he decided to groom Randy first – the aloof male donkey was likely to get bored and wander off while he attended to Peg. His new best friend was decidedly unhappy with this arrangement, however. She kept trying to get his attention by gently pushing him away. In the end it became a ridiculous tussle, and Derek found himself laughing loudly and uncontrollably. He didn't see the curtain twitch at an upstairs window, nor Catherine Wilmington-Smythe looking down on the antics with an expressionless face. She watched for a while before disappearing into the house.

Once Derek was satisfied with his handiwork, he slapped both Donkeys on the rump which sent them trotting back to the part of the field they'd come from. He then returned the brushes to the stable before going up to the house. Tentatively, he knocked on the back door. He was just about to knock again when it was suddenly thrown open.

"Heaven's man, knock if you're going to knock; don't tickle it! I wasn't sure I'd heard you. Here; like this." She proceeded to give the open door three sharp, loud raps. "There; that's what I want to hear. *Exactly* like that; understand?"

"Yes ma'am," Derek replied, nodding seriously.

"Good! Well I see you've earned your bed for tonight, so now you can clear off. Before you go, however, you'll have to do a couple of quick things for me."

"No problem at all; what do you want me to do?"

"Wait here." She retreated into the house, closing the door firmly behind her. Derek shook his head; she really was the most intimidating, eccentric, exasperating... He smiled wryly. ...and oddly kind woman he'd ever met. He turned and leant against the wall, watching the donkeys as they wandered around the field together. They were clearly inseparable.

He jumped upright as the door opened again, and a few seconds later Catherine appeared. A small folding camp stool was tucked under her left arm while in that hand she was holding a saucepan with a wooden spoon in it. Her right arm was hooked through the handle of a steaming bucket of water, with a bar of soap in that hand. A large clean rag was draped over her shoulder.

"Right then Derek," she snapped commandingly. "I made the mistake of double-salting my porridge this morning, so it's completely inedible. And since I *hate* to see food thrown away, I want you to dispose of it for me. There's a dustbin over there; you can scrape it into that." She gave him one of her thoughtful, up and down looks. "Still, if you decide you can stomach it, you're welcome to eat it. You can wash your disgusting hands first though! Here's some hot water, a bar of soap, and something to dry them on. And your face could do with a wash while you're at it. Cleanliness is next to Godliness!"

"Th..."

"And don't thank me. This is a task, not a gift!"

"Of course; I'll see to it straight away."

"Hmm. See that you do." She started to turn towards the backdoor.

A sudden thought struck Derek. "Catherine?" he asked warily.

"What?" she demanded impatiently.

"I...I don't suppose you know much about Jesus, do you?"

She froze for a moment, and then gave him such a searching, penetrating look, it left him feeling naked. "I know a bit. Why do you ask?"

"Because... because... well... I think I sort of belong to him; but I don't know anything about him."

"Don't be ridiculous man. How can you belong to him if you don't know him?"

For some reason Derek felt a burning defiance flare up inside him. *"I just do!"* he declared boldly.

Catherine studied him for a moment. "Hmm. Well you're clearly not a cretin if you could once afford a pony. Tell me Derek, how well can you read?"

"Very well. Except…" Once again, for some reason he felt very ashamed. "Except I haven't got any reading glasses."

"I see; you can't exactly *read* about him then. That is a problem. In that case, you'd be better off asking Reverend Winters. He'll be able to answer all your questions."

"I don't know why, but I don't feel I can. It's sort of…well, personal."

"Personal eh?" Catherine bit her lip thoughtfully, then appeared to make up her mind. "Very well; leave it with me. I can't promise anything, mind; but I'm sure I'll think of something or the other."

"Thank you."

"Thank me if I can help and not before. Now get on with it," she added nodding toward the bucket and the saucepan. Then she was gone to the sound of the door slamming closed. Derek took a deep breath then did as he'd been instructed.

It felt wonderful. Just the act of washing his hands and face felt so good he wanted to strip and wash everything. The thought of Catherine's wrath, however, kept that particular desire in check. When he was done washing, he picked up the saucepan and warily tasted the thick porridge. Not altogether to his surprise, it was delicious.

CHAPTER EIGHTEEN – *"ALL SCRIPTURE IS INSPIRED BY GOD AND IS USEFUL FOR TEACHING THE TRUTH... AND GIVING INSTRUCTION FOR RIGHT LIVING,"* (2 TIMOTHY 3:16)

Derek – The Fourth Prayer

The next four mornings were very much the same. He got up, he groomed the donkeys, and he knocked on the back door – three hard, sharp raps, just as he'd been instructed. Every morning Catherine appeared with the same bucket and soap. Every morning there was a breakfast which always came with some excuse or another for it being inedible; the toast is too well done, the porridge is too thick, too salty, or too sweet. Consequently, every morning he woke up feeling slightly better than the one before. Every day he went into town and managed to beg a small amount of money. And every day he tucked most of it away in his lunchbox.

His fifth morning was slightly different. The weather was gloriously sunny but rather chill with a fairly brisk northeasterly breeze. Catherine appeared at the backdoor with no bucket, and she was wearing different clothes to her norm. Although still dressed in nothing fancy, she was nonetheless much smarter than usual. Her skirt was still tweed, but she was wearing heavy denier black tights and her usual walking boots had been exchanged for well-polished women's brogues. Her ubiquitous variety of heavy sweaters had been replaced by a smart, if rather frumpy, thick knit brown cardigan over a plain white blouse. But the most startling difference was her hair. Freed from its customary ponytail, it cascaded over her shoulders, framing her face and softening her features no end.

"I'm going to church this morning and while I'm there I want you here; understood?"

"Erm... no actually. Is there something...?"

"What do you mean, no? Have the rats eaten your brains man? I mean I want you here."

"Yes, I understand that, but..."

"Don't just stand there wittering; get yourself into the kitchen."

Derek was stunned. "The kitchen?"

"Yes, the kitchen. And get a move on, I'm late enough as it is."

Without another word, Derek brushed quickly past her and into the house.

Just as he'd expected, it was larger than most kitchens, and he wasn't altogether surprised at its lack of modernity. There was an old-fashioned range, a huge Belfast-type sink, and row upon row of farmhouse-style cupboards. A deep reddish-brown flagstone floor added to the old-fashioned look, as did the large, plain wooden table in the middle of the room. Derek wondered why on Earth it needed six of the bare wooden chairs arranged around it. Did this woman ever have company? A large plate of bacon and eggs sat tantalisingly on a tray in the middle of the table with a smaller plate of thick-cut bread and butter beside it.

Catherine pointed to the corner of the room nearest the backdoor. "Right; there's *two* buckets this time. Since I'll be away all morning you can take your rags off and give yourself a proper wash. You stink like a sloppy farmer's pigsty and it makes me feel ill. I suggest you give your rags a wash too – the sight of the major's old coat rubbing against them makes me shudder. And since I'm not too sure they'll survive the ordeal I went back to the charity shop and bought a few useful items. They're all in that plastic sack there. Have a look through and see if there's anything you want. And you can wipe that look off your face; they're not a gift, I expect you to pay for them."

Derek's face fell. "Erm... I'm sorry but..."

"Good heavens man, don't tell me you haven't got *any* money."

"A little bit, but that charity shop's prices are very high – this coat was twenty pounds."

"I know perfectly well how much it cost; but that was *their* price. Since most of what's in the bag was donated by me in the first place, I negotiated a good discount. I've pinned a ticket with the new price onto each garment."

Derek smiled to himself – he could just imagine how those negotiations had gone.

"There's a towel in there too, but that *is* free since it'll help wash some the stink off you – so it's for my benefit and not yours."

"Th..." The glare Catherine gave him left the 'thank you' dead in his throat.

"Right then; as I said, I'm running late and I haven't got time to eat my breakfast. You might as well have it – but you can eat it *outside*."

"Yes ma'am; right away." As quick as he could, he put the buckets, soap, stool, and bag outside the back door. He then turned to see Catherine standing in the doorway, the breakfast tray in her hands. He was surprised to see there was also a steaming mug of tea on it.

"Wash your hands and eat this while it's still hot," She said in a flat, brisk voice. "And *don't* break the crockery!"

"I won't."

"Hmm. Leave the tray at the door here. You can perform your ablutions in the stable. Use the tap at the water trough to rinse your clothes – not *into* the trough! There's a hosepipe lying beside it."

"Of course."

Catherine looked at the sky. "It's a perfect drying day, so if your rags do survive their ordeal, you can peg them out on the washing line. There's some washing powder in the bag... I assume you do know how to wash clothes?" she added peering at him questioningly.

"Well... I used to use a washing machine – but let's face it, it's pretty obvious how..."

"Not for a man," she interrupted abruptly. "When you've finished washing yourself, give your clothes a good soaking with the hosepipe and then put them in the bucket with your dirty water, but *without* the powder. Give them a good pounding with a broom handle then take 'em out and use the hosepipe on them again. Then put them in the second bucket with the powder and pound them again. Rinse, wring, and hang them to dry. As I say, I don't expect them to survive."

"I'll have a good look through the bag and see what I can afford."

"Good man. Right, I'm off now. I'll be back about one o'clock so make sure you're decent by then. I'll come and collect the money for the clothes you've bought once I've changed. Well don't just stand there man; take the tray!"

As soon as he had his hands on it, she whirled round and was gone, slamming the door as seemed to be her usual custom. Somewhat dumbfounded, Derek stood looking at the back door for a moment or two; but then hunger overcame his amazement. Completely forgetting to wash his hands, he settled himself down on the stool, and with the tray balanced on his lap, he demolished the three eggs and four rashers of bacon, mopping his plate with the last piece of bread. The tea was strong and sweet –

just the way he liked it. With breakfast over, he set about the rest of his tasks.

He took everything to the stable and then opened the plastic sack. As she'd said, on top of the clothes was a large bath towel and a little plastic tub which he assumed held the washing powder. There was also a flannel, and since it had no price ticket, he assumed that it was included with the towel. He quickly stripped naked and set about performing his ablutions.

It was wonderful. He rubbed and scrubbed himself all over and even washed his hair. Once clean, a wicked grin appeared on his face. Wrapping himself in the towel, he walked outside to the water trough. After a quick look around, he threw the towel aside and turned the hose on himself. The two donkeys stood watching his antics from a safe distance, their faces wearing an expression of faint curiosity. He couldn't help letting out a loud, sharp exclamation as the freezing water cascaded over his head and body. He could only bear it for a few seconds, but when he was finished, he burst out laughing. He retrieved the towel and ran back to the shelter of the stable.

As he dried himself, shivering and shaking with cold, he laughed and laughed, shouting, "Thank you Jesus" between guffaws. When he was dry, he wrapped himself in his blanket, threw his tattered and holey sweater, tee-shirt, trousers, and underwear into the bucket, and attacked them with the stable broom. Catherine was partly right. While his trousers and frayed jumper remained intact, his tee-shirt and underpants did not. After hanging the surviving garments on the washing line near the house, he delved into the sack to see what he could find.

There was a pair of jeans, a shirt, a tee-shirt, two thick sweaters, two pairs of underpants, and a pair of long johns. Amazingly, they all looked to be close to his size – but then again, if like his coat they'd belonged to the major, they would be. But what about the price? A hand written ticket was attached to each one with a safety pin. Once again, he burst out laughing. The most expensive item was the pair of jeans. They were priced at an extortionate fifty pence. The sweaters were thirty pence each, while everything else was just ten pence. The whole ensemble came to a ridiculously cheap £1.60; and he had exactly £6.60 saved up in his lunchbox!

Carefully, he removed the tickets and threaded them all onto one of the safety pins. He dressed himself in his new jeans and tee-shirt, along with the smarter of the two sweaters. His new underwear felt unbearably comfortable, while the long johns certainly helped to warm up his legs. Eventually he sat down amongst the straw that made his bed and let out a huge and satisfied sigh. He didn't care what Catherine said, when she came home, he was going to give her one big thank...

Suddenly it dawned on him exactly where she'd said she was going. Church; she was a Christian; she was a follower of Jesus – the same Jesus to whom he'd given his life. His eyes fell on the ripped and sodden remains of his old clothes and he burst into tears. But they were tears of gratitude, tears of love, and tears of hope.

* * *

He was grooming the donkeys again when Catherine returned. He heard the Land Rover pull up beside the house and grinned. He couldn't wait to see her reaction to his transformation, nor the look on her face when he handed her the money. He had the one pound sixty ready in his pocket along with the tickets and the safety pins. His excitement mounted unbearably as the time passed, and it was a full twenty minutes before the back door opened and she appeared. She'd obviously taken the time to change into her usual apparel, and she had something tucked under her arm. He'd dragged out the grooming waiting for her; but then that was something the donkeys seemed to enjoy. Two long sessions in one day was clearly a welcome treat.

"Derek; here!" Catherine called as though he were a dog; and obediently, he obeyed.

"Yes Catherine?" he said as he trotted up to the back door. The thing under her arm turned out to be an old square biscuit tin.

Catherine eyed him critically up and down. "Better," she said with a sharp nod. "Money?" she added holding out her hand.

"Money," Derek confirmed pulling the coins from his pocket and handing them over.

Catherine slipped them into her pocket without even glancing at them.

"And here's the tickets and pins."

She took them absently then gave him a penetrating look. "You were asking about Jesus."

His heart leapt. "Yes, I was. I want to..."

"Were you serious?"

"Yes; very serious."

"And you say you belong to him, but can't exactly say why?"

For some reason Derek's heart was thumping in his chest. "Yes...no... I mean..." He dried up, unsure of how to express his thoughts.

"Come on, spit it out." Suddenly her voice changed and became almost kindly – almost. "I won't bite."

He gulped, took a deep breath, and then told her about Kings Cross Station.

"Hmm, I see. Very well; in that case this is yours." She handed him the biscuit tin.

Puzzled, he took it from her and pulled off the lid. Inside was a book – a brand new book at that. The cover had a close-up picture of a calm blue-green sea with the book's title boldly written in large white letters: 'THE MESSAGE'. Beneath that in smaller letters it read: 'THE BIBLE IN CONTEMPORARY LANGUAGE'. Lying on top of the book was a large magnifying glass. He stared at it numbly, unable to comprehend what he'd done to deserve such kindness.

"Of course, it's not what I call a *proper* Bible," Catherine said, back to her usual clipped and curt manner. "Paraphrases everything – appallingly, in my opinion. Still, it's easy to read and gets the main message across – hence the title, I suppose."

"It's...it's wonderful." A terrible thought flashed through his mind and he looked at her in horror. "How much will it cost me; I've only got..."

"Don't be ridiculous man; this one *is* a gift. At least the book is, the magnifying glass is mine. You can borrow it until you get some reading glasses. It should be good enough for now."

Tears began to well up in Derek's eyes, something that seemed to horrify Catherine. His mouth opened and closed, but he could find no words to express his gratitude.

"You can stay in the stable this afternoon and read it; I recommend you begin in the New Testament at Matthew chapter one, verse eighteen. That's where you'll start to learn about Jesus. Matthew, Mark, Luke, and John – they're the four gospels. The rest of the Bible is just as relevant, but for now, it's Jesus you need to know about."

Still Derek could think of nothing worthy enough to say.

"Well go on man; off you go. Start reading!"

Derek blinked once or twice then replaced the lid. He almost ran back to the stable, unable to decide whether to cry or to whoop with joy. In the end it came out as a mixture of both.

Behind him, Catherine watched him gambol across the field with a stern, disapproving expression on her face. Suddenly, a brief and gentle smile lit up her eyes; but a second later it was gone and she spun around and marched back into the house.

Derek reached the stable and dropped onto his straw bed. With trembling hands, he opened the lid and took out the book. He was about to open it when he saw his dirt-ingrained fingers. Although he knew his hands were clean – especially after this morning's shenanigans – two years of filth had left their mark. Perhaps it was a fitting metaphor. Perhaps he himself still looked unclean, but had somehow been made pure by the love of Jesus. Eagerly he opened the book and by using the magnifying glass, he soon found the page Catherine had suggested. The section from Matthew chapter one verse 18 onward was subtitled, *The Birth of Jesus.* He took a deep breath and began to read.

"The birth of Jesus took place like this. His mother, Mary was engaged..."

CHAPTER NINETEEN – "A TIME TO WEEP AND A TIME TO LAUGH." (ECCLESIASTES 3:4)

Derek – The Fourth Prayer

Derek peered deep into Reverend John's eyes, half hidden in the shadow of the street lamps' weak light. Now that the generator was silent, the tent's light was out, adding to the dim and sombre mood in the air. His insides writhed with the agony of indecision. Cath had been absolutely clear. "Tell no one," she'd commanded forcefully. "If you do, you'll be out!" And he'd obeyed her with absolute, unequivocal, and total compliance. Not a word about any of his association with her had passed his lips. But surely this situation was another matter. Surely, she would understand him revealing his secret to Reverend Winters and his wife.

"It's a long story," he eventually replied. "But I sort of... Well, I kind of live at her place – but I'm not supposed to tell anyone that, so please keep it just between us."

"Our lips are sealed," John reassured him. "I tell you what, finish helping us pack up and I'll give you a lift. You can tell me as much as you want to on the way."

Derek considered it for a moment then nodded. "Thanks; it's a bit late to walk there anyway."

It didn't take long to finish taking down the tent and to pack it into the van. Jenny responded to the news of Sticks' death with an apparent lack of emotion that masked the true depth of feeling John could see she was hiding. She gave John and Anne a big hug and a kiss, and then after just a slight hesitation, she gave Derek a quick squeeze too. They all then climbed wearily into their respective vehicles. As Derek got into John's Corsa, he glanced at Sticks' sleeping bag.

"What are you planning to do with that?" he asked casually.

John blew out his cheeks. "I'm not sure. Why, do you want it?"

Derek shook his head. "No, I don't need it. I just thought maybe Cath should have it."

"Why is that?"

"Dunno; I just do"

John looked at him for a moment. There was definitely something more to it than just a vague feeling, but the old man's face was impossible to read. And when the car's interior light went out, it was impossible even to see. John watched the van and Anne's car pull away and decided to give Derek a chance to open up. For a long while they sat in silence; but for some reason it wasn't a strained one. John was sure the old man would eventually break the silence, but when he did, his words came as a surprise.

"Did you know that I'm a Christian?"

"No, I didn't; but then most people were christened as babies."

There was another short silence. "I don't mean that. I mean I've given myself to Jesus; I said the sinner's prayer and I meant it."

"I'm sorry Derek; I didn't realise. It's wonderful news though."

"Hmm."

"I haven't seen you at church with Mrs Wilmington-Smythe, or do you go somewhere else."

"No; I don't go to church."

"Oh. If you don't mind me asking, is there any particular reason?"

Derek snorted derisively. "Look at me. Do you think your congregation would welcome me? Cath has hinted that I should go, but I'm pretty sure she doesn't want me going *with* her, if you know what I mean."

"Derek, the Bible says..."

"I know what it says, Rev; I read it every day. I'm just not sure your congregation knows what it says."

"Oh Derek; of course they..." John stopped in mid-sentence. Did they? Did they really? An image of them all sitting in front of him that very morning flashed into his mind. It was an affluent congregation and a surprisingly large one in this day and age. They were all very smartly dressed, and many of their clothes were designer and exclusive. The collection was always generously large, but was that as far as their charity went? Oh, he was pretty sure they all subscribed their two pounds a month to Save the Children or Water Aid. Maybe some had even sponsored a child in some poverty-stricken part of the world. All of that was highly commendable, but he also knew there had been rumblings about the soup kitchen. And he had an uncomfortable feeling that something wasn't quite right in his congregation. Maybe Derek was right; maybe they would be unkind to him.

"So how do you manage to worship God? It must be very difficult."

Derek gave a sardonic laugh. "Why would you ask that? How could it be more difficult than what went before? I worship our Lord every day on my own; I don't need anyone else to help me do that."

John sighed. "You know Derek, I believe there's an awful lot to you, and I would love to know some of it. Please, my friend, tell me what you can. I imagine there's even some lessons I can learn from your story."

For a moment there was no reply, but then came a quiet, "Maybe, maybe not."

"At the very least let me pray with you. Sometimes it helps to have someone to pray with. Do you pray regularly?"

This time Derek's laugh was a good one. It was soft and pleasant to hear. "My dear Rev; of course I pray. I pray when I wake up; I pray when I wash; I pray when I eat; I pray when I read my Bible... and I say a small prayer for others like me. I pray all day and every day."

John was staggered. He'd had no idea that this old and fragile vagrant, this beggar with his long, untidy wisps of grey hair and wild, untamed beard could be so devout a Christian.

A sudden thought struck him. "And what do you ask from our Lord?"

"Ask for?" Derek replied sounding a little shocked. "Why would I ask for anything more than he's given me? Other than his constant guidance, I have everything I need. I have enough food to keep me alive and I have enough clothes to keep me warm – and I even have the same home as our Lord did when he was born. Whenever I pray I have only one thought, only one thing to say, and that is, *Thank You*."

John closed his eyes and drew a soft breath. He suddenly felt very humbled. "Please Derek," he said a few moments later. Tell me something about yourself." And then to his amazement, Derek did.

He gave the briefest description of his rise and fall; he told of the alcohol, of how close he'd been to the end. But he told him in great detail about the desperate prayer on the steps of Jenson's, and of how God's firm hand had set him on a new path. He even told him about how he'd come by the train ticket to Rewford. His voice became choked with emotion when he recounted the part about Rachael and the sinner's prayer. And then he told John about the jacket and the wallet he'd found in the pocket.

"Oh, my Lord!" exclaimed John. "How did you resist the temptation?"

Derek thought for a moment. "I'm not sure. I guess *HE* told me to."

Then the story continued, but when it came to the wages for his bed, John burst out laughing.

"What?" Derek asked defensively.

"I'm sorry," John replied, quickly regaining control of himself. "But honestly Derek; Donkeys don't need to be groomed – at least very seldom. They tend to groom each other. And I'm certain that Mrs... I mean Catherine, would have known that all along. It sounds like she's been playing some kind of trick on you."

To John's horror, Derek immediately hid his face his hands and began to cry. He cursed himself for his lack of tact, for he'd probably just destroyed the nearest thing to friendship Derek had.

But he was wrong; he was very wrong. It had suddenly become clear to Derek the full extent of Cath's kindness. By pointlessly making him groom the donkeys she'd given him the self-respect of work and wages, and she'd provided him with two very dear and unjudging friends as well. Then Derek couldn't hold it in any longer. "Thank you Jesus; thank you Jesus; Oh thank you Jesus!"

And then in a burst of inspiration, John understood. With a smile and a tear of empathy trickling down his cheek, he started the car and took Derek home.

CHAPTER TWENTY –
"THERE ARE THOSE WHO REBEL AGAINST THE LIGHT."
(JOB 24:13)

Betrayal

Stick's funeral had been a pathetic and lonely affair. John had conducted the service at the crematorium in Frinton – a service attended by a paltry four people. Catherine was there of course, as were Derek and Jerry. The fourth attendee had been Father Jolly, the only representative from Saint Mary's Children's Home who was available. The priest had displayed a deep and profound grief over the poor boy's fate, but something about it didn't ring true with John. Catherine had certainly given him the cold shoulder, while Derek had spoken to him only when necessary. Jerry on the other hand had appeared quite at ease with him. Yet there was something about the ex-soldier's affability that had made John's blood run cold. It carried an underlying threat more dangerous than even the most menacing kind of belligerence. Jolly, however, had seemed oblivious to it all.

There had been no autopsy and no inquest. Sticks' death had been attributed to natural causes. Heart failure brought on by sepsis, exposure, and malnutrition. His identity had also been quickly tracked down. Catherine had recognised the boy's accent, which gave the police an idea of where to search the missing persons register. Dean James had popped up almost immediately. And so, just two weeks and three days after John had carried the dying boy into Accident and Emergency, Dean James' remains had been cremated. The whole affair had been paid for by an anonymous donation – although John had a sneaking suspicion about who the unknown benefactor might be.

It was now four weeks and two days since Dean's cremation. It was almost two o'clock and John was sitting at the desktop in his office trying to write his sermon for the coming Sunday. No matter what theme he started with, however, the words became harder and harder to find. Every time he had to give up and start again. He would say an earnest prayer asking the Spirit to guide him, and then off he would go on another tack which in turn would soon grind to the same stuttering halt. He was sure he would soon wear out the delete key on the keyboard.

Of course, it didn't help his concentration knowing that Stuffy would be arriving soon. The bishop had phoned yesterday morning to arrange the visit. When asked the purpose of the appointment, Stuffy had been curiously vague. "Best to discuss it in person," was all he would say. John had a very bad feeling about it all.

He was just about to begin his sixth attempt at a sermon when the doorbell rang. John looked at his watch. The damned man was fifteen minutes early; and Stuffy was always and scrupulously ten minutes late. John's disquiet reached unpleasant new heights. He sent the computer to sleep and slowly rose from his chair. He heard Anne answer the door and could just about make out her welcome and Stuffy's unintelligible reply. After taking a deep breath, he left the office and went to greet his unwelcome visitor. He knew Anne would be showing him into the sitting room.

"Richard," John said brightly, holding out his hand. The bishop shook it briefly and nodded.

"John," he replied somewhat sombrely. "Shall we sit?"

"Of course, please do. Anne dear, could you rustle up some tea and biscuits?"

"No not for me," the bishop said hurriedly as he sat down in one of the two armchairs. "This shouldn't take long." He gave Anne a lingering look that made it clear she was not included in the upcoming discussion.

"Right then," she said with a winning smile. "I'll leave you to it. If you change your mind, Richard, just tell John to give me a shout. I'm going to put the kettle on just in case." With another dazzling smile, she turned and breezed out of the room.

John took a seat in the armchair facing the bishop. "So, Richard, what's this all about? You were very cryptic on the phone yesterday."

The Right Reverend Richard Anderson was nowhere near as imposing as his title. In fact, it would be hard to find a more nondescript, unremarkable person in the whole country. Everything about him was average apart from his manner. He always spoke in a slow and deliberate voice as though he here picking each word with careful precision. His entire mien was so aloof, it had quickly earned him the nickname 'Stuffy' from Anne. This not-so-endearing attitude, however, hid a genuinely caring personality. But his absolute dedication to efficiency made his better qualities rather difficult to find.

"Yes, I appreciate I must have caused some trepidation on your part, but this really is a rather delicate subject to broach."

"So I gathered. What's going on, Richard; is it something dire?"

Bishop Anderson closed his eyes for a moment as he gathered his thoughts. When he opened them, he leaned back in the chair and steepled his fingers. "I'm afraid there have been complaints, John – lots of complaints."

"Complaints? Complaints about what?"

"About your... how do you call it, kitchen?"

John frowned. "The soup kitchen? What sort of complaints?"

"It seems people feel it has attracted, how shall we say, the wrong elements to town?"

"The wrong elements?" John could feel his cheeks glowing red with indignation. "So the destitute and hopeless are the wrong elements, are they?"

"Now, now, John," Richard replied holding up a placating hand. "Please don't take offense. But you must understand that people are concerned for their safety. While I'm sure some of your clientele are deserving of your charity, most are alcoholics or drug addicts; and some have caused great offense. And their numbers have grown exponentially."

"I'd hardly call sixteen or so 'exponential'. And these are exactly the people we need to reach. Did not Christ himself sit down with sinners?"

"That's not the point, and you know it."

"That *is* the point!"

"You're making this very difficult you know."

"Good!" John cried, getting to his feet. "It needs to be difficult."

"John, please. I'm sure you can appreciate the people's concerns. One of the erm... *women*, has actually stripped naked in the street – several times in fact."

"Yes, I know; and that *woman*, has a name. Elizabeth Johnson; although everyone calls her Batty Betty."

"Name or not, we can't have anyone running naked through the streets of Rewford!"

"Well she won't be doing it anymore," stated John defiantly. "I became aware of her problems and alerted the health authority. She is now receiving the care she so obviously needed. And that, bishop, is thanks to the kitchen."

Richard looked up at him with a small, beatific smile on his lips. "John, John; I understand what you're saying, and I know that you're upset. I know how passionate you are about this project. But I also understand the concerns of the people who have written to the council." He leaned forward and gave John a severe look. "There's been a petition you know."

"I've heard nothing from the council. Why, have they written to you?"

Richard looked a little embarrassed. "Well... erm... no, not as such."

"So what's the problem then?"

"There have been rumblings within the church – and not just at Saint Andrew's; several of the congregations hereabouts have put in a complaint. Even some from the Grange Methodist Church have raised their objections. You have to realise, this a wealthy area; people aren't used to this type of people."

John was stunned. "You mean it's the *Christian* community that's complaining? Followers of our Lord Jesus Christ begrudge a hot meal to those in need?"

"You're oversimplifying it," Richard replied, his cheeks also beginning to turn red.

"That's because it *is* simple. Don't they realise that one of those 'undesirables' – a seventeen-year-old boy – died a few weeks ago. I'm sorry Richard, but with due respect, it's up to you to make sure the congregations are made aware of the need to be more chari..."

"The decision has been made, John," Richard interrupted sharply. "Your kitchen experiment must end at once. I'll give you this weekend to let your lost causes know it's closing down. But Sunday *will* be the last time they are fed, is that clear?"

John could find no words to reply. He stood open mouthed with shock. It wasn't the secular authorities closing him down, it was his own church.

"I said, is that clear?" demanded Richard.

John swallowed bitterly. "Yes, Bishop Anderson," he grated between clenched teeth.

"Very well then. I'll leave you to get on with whatever it is you're doing, and then you can start making the arrangements as soon as possible." He got to his feet and started towards the door. As he passed John he stopped and gave him a mollifying smile. "Remember, John; you must put the needs of your own flock first."

John watched the bishop as he went to the sitting room door. "Right Reverend Anderson," he said in a low voice, addressing him by his formal title.

"Yes John?" Richard asked turning around. His features still wore the placating smile.

"They're not *my* flock, nor even *your* flock; they are Christ's."

The bishop's face fell and flushed an angry red. He glared at John for a moment before spinning on his heels and stalking out of the house.

John listened to him go, his breathing heavy with constricted fury. The betrayal was unbearable and made everything seem so pointless. But then he remembered Derek. He hadn't seen him since the funeral; but after talking to him and Catherine there, it seemed he was still making good progress. *Now there is a Christian,* he thought. *Humble, devout, and with a consuming hunger to learn more about the Lord.* The kitchen had helped at least one man on his way to salvation.

He suddenly laughed. "Thank you, Jesus!" he shouted at the top of his voice. "Thank you, Lord!"

"John!" Anne cried as she appeared in the doorway. "What on Earth's happened? Was it good news after all?"

"No, my love," John replied still beaming. "It was the worst. Stuffy is shutting the kitchen down."

"Then why are you so happy? Have you gone mad?"

John rushed over to her and swept her up into his arms. She gasped as he swung her into the room. "Because my darling, as our Lord himself said: *'I say to you that there will be more joy in heaven over one sinner who repents than over ninety-nine just persons who need no repentance.'"*

"What on Earth are you talking about?"

"Love and salvation, my sweet; love and salvation. And I now know *exactly* what topic Sunday's sermon will be about; and they aren't going to like it one bit!"

CHAPTER TWENTY-ONE –
"AND WHOEVER GIVES ONE OF THESE LITTLE ONES ONLY A CUP OF COLD WATER IN THE NAME OF A DISCIPLE, ASSUREDLY, I SAY TO YOU, HE SHALL BY NO MEANS LOSE HIS REWARD." (MATTHEW 10:42)

A Sermon of Shame

John stood in the pulpit and surveyed the congregation. As good as it was to see his own church so full, he could not help feeling a tiny pang of sorrow for some other churches in the country. He knew that many were struggling to maintain their numbers. Although both of Rewford's churches were always well attended, they were often the exception to the rule. Only on special occasions were the church pews filled in a lot of other towns and cities. Weddings always drew the biggest crowd of course, but a good baptism could also be well attended. Funerals were...

He stopped himself short; that was too sore a subject, and he would have enough trouble holding it together through this particular sermon as it was. And since it could well be one of his last – a decision that had been drawing near for some time – he wanted his performance to be a good one.

As the silence continued and the seconds mounted, an air of impatience began to ripple through the congregation, punctuated by the occasional irritated cough. *Good! Make them wait.* His eyes searched their faces. He looked at their fine clothes and expensive jewellery. They were all so very, very respectable. It was the same every Sunday; they attended, they sang the hymns, they made the correct responses in the liturgy, they knelt in prayer; and of course, the collection plate was always *very* full; but now he was sure. Saint Andrew's Church, Rewford had a problem; a very serious problem; and it was a problem he was determined to lay bare.

It was a congregation with more than its fair share of pensioners – wealthy pensioners, but there were a good many young, well-off middle-class families too. Indeed, in the front row to his left was the newest and youngest member. Three-month-old Russell was peacefully asleep in his father's arms. He really was a happy and peaceful little baby. His mother sat beside her husband with her usual extremely pious, if now slightly puzzled, look on her deceptively young and pretty face. Barring only a handful, that same piety was reflected in most of the faces before him – indeed, there was always a faint yet overpowering whiff of sanctimony amongst them all.

In the one empty row right at the back, Catherine Wilmington-Smythe sat in her usual lonely spot; except this time, she was not alone. She was accompanied by a very smartly dressed man whom John didn't recognise. His hair was so closely cropped, he was near to being bald. He looked at most to be in his early fifties. His smart blue, pinstripe suit was most business like, as was his crisp white shirt. Only his candy-pink and white striped tie lifted the severity of his mien. On the other side of the central aisle sat an even lonelier figure; and it was someone John was happier to see there than almost anyone. It was Jerry. He looked uncomfortably out of place in his crumpled and dirty coat, although at least his face was clean and his greasy hair had been combed. John was determined to catch him before he could make his escape after the service.

Behind him, John could feel the eyes of the choir burning into the back of his neck, while Graeme the organist gave a very pointed and impatient cough.

John drew a deep breath; a moment's hesitation before setting off on this journey to an alarmingly unfamiliar destination. Then Anne caught his eye. She was sitting in the front row to his right alongside three of her best friends from the women's committee. Clearly, she understood his qualms, but her reassuring smile and nod of encouragement immediately overcame his doubts.

He began his sermon.

"What is a Christian?" he asked rhetorically. "Most would say a believer in Christ, for the most famous scripture in the world – John 3:16 – says,

"*'For God so loved the world that he gave his only Son, that whoever **believes** in him should not perish but have eternal life.'*

"And then a little further on at verse thirty-six:

"*'The one who **believes** in the Son has eternal life.'*

"Now I know every one of you here believes in him, am I right?"

There followed a satisfying number of nods around the church.

"But what does it mean to believe in him? Does a demon believe that Jesus is the son of God? He does more than just believe it; he *knows* it! So if the Devil and his demons believe in him, are they Christians? Of course not! And I'm pretty sure I haven't seen too many demons in church lately."

A lot of people smiled at the last bit. John wondered how long those smiles would last.

"So, what is the difference between a demon's belief and a Christian's belief? Faith? Of course, faith; but the book of James says that faith without deeds is worthless. But on the other hand, Saint Paul says that you cannot earn salvation through deeds; and that it is only through the grace of our Lord Jesus Christ that we are saved. Is this a contradiction? Not at all! When we receive Christ as our Saviour, we are filled with the Holy Spirit. As Jesus told Nicodemus, we are born again. And we are born a new person full of the fruits of the Spirit.

These fruits are: *love, joy, peace, patience, kindness, goodness, faithfulness, gentleness, and self-control.* With all these, the deeds spring forth as inevitably as warmth comes from the sun. So, it inescapably follows that if there are no deeds, no works of love –

that is charity – there is no Holy Spirit, and therefore the faith is dead.

But that raises another question: what are the deeds that validate our faith? I tell you, my brothers and sisters, those deeds are many, but they all have one wellspring; and that wellspring is love.

"The word 'love' was often once translated as charity, which I imagine most of you already knew – at least I hope you did. And I imagine most of you are *very* charitable. I know the collection plate here is always full, and I know the church's charities do well by you. And I'm sure a lot of the 'two pounds a month' donation pleas we see on the television are well subscribed to as well."

This time there were even more nods; but too many were accompanied by a self-satisfied smile for John's liking.

"These are all worthwhile charities, and I commend all of you who support them. And I would encourage all of you who don't to consider donating what you can as well. Jesus said that the greatest commandment is to love God with all your heart, soul, and mind; and the second, like it, is to love your neighbor as yourself. When asked who exactly your neighbor is, Jesus told the parable of the Good Samaritan. I'm sure everyone, apart from little

Russell here (more smiles) knows that parable; but here's a brief refresher.

"A certain man – a Jew – is beaten and robbed of everything including his clothes. He is then left for dead at the roadside. A priest and a Levite – two of the most righteous of the man's countrymen – metaphorically step over his stricken form. But a Samaritan – a people detested by the Jews – rescues him. He puts him up at an inn, pays for his food and medicines, and promises to check in on his return journey to make sure that he'd left enough money to cover the expenses. Jesus makes it clear that the hated Samaritan is the man's neighbor, and not the highly respected priest and Levite."

John paused and glared accusingly around at the sea of faces looking up at him. "Tell me all of you, do you consider yourself to be like the Good Samaritan, or the Levite? Are you a good neighbour, *or a hypocrite?*"

By the look on most people's faces, they did indeed consider themselves to be Good Samaritans. John let a few moments of silence pass before carrying on in a more sombre tone.

"Exactly seven weeks ago today, I carried a very sick young man – little more than a boy – into the local Accident and Emergency. I'd been sitting talking to him only minutes beforehand.

Distressingly, he died less than an hour later. Sticks is the name we knew him by; he wouldn't tell us his real name. All I knew was that he was destitute, homeless, and helpless. The soup kitchen I ran with the help of a few volunteers from this church and from the Grange Methodists, was the only certainty in that poor boy's life. Unfortunately for him, it wasn't enough."

There was now a measure of discomfort spreading around the church.

"Since his death, we've found out a great deal more about young Sticks. We now know that he was just seventeen when he died, and that he'd been sleeping rough on Rewford's streets for a whole year. Exactly why he came here is a mystery. He certainly wasn't drawn here by the soup kitchen because he ran away from a children's home in Northumberland a few days before it opened."

Out of the corner of his eye he saw little Russell's mother stiffen. When he looked at her, he saw that her face had turned white.

"The saddest thing of all was his funeral. Only four mourners. Just four people to grieve over the loss of poor Sticks.

"Tell me honestly, brothers and sisters, how many of you – you who imagine yourselves to be Good Samaritans – stepped over him in the street? How many of you walked past him like a priest or a Levite? Did any one of you give him so much as a friendly smile? How many of you can say that Dean James received your charity – that is, *your love*?"

Russell's mother climbed slowly to her feet. Her face was ashen, and her expression was blank with shock. John had only ever seen such a terrible look in someone's eyes once before. That had been at a road accident where a man had just mown down two little girls with his car.

To her husband's dismay, Julie Hatcher then turned and walked mechanically down the Aisle towards the exit. Gary Hatcher watched her go, confusion etched deep into his features. A moment later, he too got up, and with little Russell in his arms, he hurried after his wife.

For a moment John watched them leave, a puzzled and concerned frown furrowing his brow. He made a mental note to visit the Hatchers sometime soon. With much nudging and whispering, the congregation also watched them go. But John still had an important point to make.

"I repeat my question," he said forcefully, once again gaining everyone's attention. "How many of you ignored Dean's plight? Let me ask you another question: how many of you complained about the soup kitchen that actually *did* help? How many of you signed the petition demanding that it be closed? Well, congratulations; you have succeeded. Tonight – just seventeen days before Christmas – is the very last night it will serve food to those who most need it."

Several men and women hung their heads in shame, but to John's horror, there were many times their number who had a satisfied smirk on their lips. He wondered if he could manage to wipe it off.

"I want to close this sermon by reading a warning from our Lord Jesus Christ himself. That warning is found at Matthew twenty-five, verses thirty-four to thirty-six.

'"Then the king will say to those at his right hand, 'Come, you that are blessed by my Father, inherit the kingdom prepared for you from the foundation of the world; for I was hungry and you gave me food, I was thirsty and you gave me something to drink, I was a stranger and you welcomed me, I was naked and you gave me clothing, I was sick and you took care of me, I was in prison and you visited me.' Then the righteous will answer him, 'Lord, when was it that we saw you hungry and gave you food, or thirsty and gave you something to drink? And when was it that we saw you a stranger and welcomed you, or naked and gave you clothing? And when was it that we saw you sick or in prison and visited you?' And the king will answer them, 'Truly I tell you, just as you did it to one

*of the least of these who are members of my family, you
did it to me.'*

*"Then he will say to those at his left hand, 'You that are
accursed, depart from me into the eternal fire prepared for
the devil and his angels; for I was hungry and you gave me
no food, I was thirsty and you gave me nothing to drink, I
was a stranger and you did not welcome me, naked and
you did not give me clothing, sick and in prison and you
did not visit me.' Then they also will answer, 'Lord, when
was it that we saw you hungry or thirsty or a stranger or
naked or sick or in prison, and did not take care of
you?' Then he will answer them, 'Truly I tell you, just as
you did not do it to one of the least of these, you did not do
it to me.' And these will go away into eternal punishment,
but the righteous into eternal life.'"*

John looked up from his Bible and studied every
single face. Many, he noticed, could now not meet his
eye. He then launched into his parting salvo.

"Please, do not think that I am judging you – any
of you. That is not my place. But I *am* here to teach
you and to guide you. Do you really think that all the
good charities you support or all the good works you
like to pat yourselves on the back for are enough?
Brothers and sisters, they are not!" He held up his
Bible and waved it in the air. "Even if you know every
word in here by heart, it isn't enough. What do you

profit by knowing the book if you do not know the author? You MUST get to know him. And once you truly know him, you'll realise that love does not end when you exit the doors of this church and then begin again in some far-off foreign land. When you know him, you will realise that; and only then will he know you."

He went back to his Bible and flipped through the pages to Matthew chapter seven, and starting at verse twenty-one, he began to read.

"Not everyone who says to me, 'Lord, Lord,' shall enter the kingdom of heaven, but he who does the will of my Father who is in heaven. On that day many will say to me, 'Lord, Lord, did we not prophesy in your name, and cast out demons in your name, and do many mighty works in your name?' And then will I declare to them, 'I never knew you; depart from me, you evildoers.'

One last time, he glared around the congregation. "There endeth the lesson," he said coldly. Then in his usual pleasant voice he added, "Communion will now follow."

To the sound of much vexed muttering, he turned and left the pulpit.

* * *

For some reason, John wasn't as popular as usual after the service. Almost nobody came up to him and thanked him or congratulated him on a wonderful sermon. A few did, but they seemed nervous about doing so as if concerned about what their outraged fellows might think. And so, to the powerful sound of Graeme's organ playing, they made their hurried exit from the church. It was therefore easy to make his way to the back towards Jerry. His fears that Jerry might leave before he got to him were unfounded. His quarry was standing by the wall near the door, engaged in deep conversation with Catherine's business-like companion. Both men had their backs to him, while Catherine's friend had a friendly hand on Jerry's shoulder. Keeping his eyes fixed firmly on the two men, John pushed his way through the milling congregation towards them. Suddenly, his shoulder was gripped by a firm hand and he was spun around to be confronted by Catherine herself.

"I want a word with you," she said bluntly above the echoing music.

"Certainly," he replied hurriedly. "But I need to catch..."

"I want a word with you *now*!" she interrupted firmly, drawing more than a few disapproving looks from those around them.

"Catherine, I have to speak with Jerry before he leaves."

"Of course you do; but *I* will speak to you first."

John sighed. This formidable woman would not be denied. "Very well, but please be quick."

"I will be as quick or as long it takes. Now, since you're closing down the kitchen, you won't be requiring the food van – am I right?"

"Erm... no, I've advertised it..."

"Good. I will purchase it from you. My charity manager over there will discuss the details with you in a moment. I take it the sale will include the tent – as you like to call it – along with the generator and food stock?"

John was flabbergasted. "Erm..."

"Good grief man, why does everyone begin their sentences with that ridiculous sound. Does the sale include everything or not?"

"It wasn't going to, but it could be arranged if..."

"Good. The manager will speak to you about it shortly."

"But I don't quite understand; why would you want to buy it?"

Catherine gave him one of her withering glares. "Really, reverend; I thought you had more intelligence. Obviously, I intend to continue your work. The kitchen will stay open."

Her voice was brusque and loud and there were at least two or three horrified gasps from those within earshot.

For a few moments John was speechless. Utter confusion, gratitude, and hope swirled wildly around inside him rendering coherent speech impossible.

"Hmm; cat got your tongue, I see."

A sudden thought struck him. "All our customers have been told that tonight will be the last night. Some of them are distraught; and to be honest, I'm worried about what they might do."

"Which is why the news should to be spread amongst them as soon as possible. That is going to be Jerry's task – if he agrees to it. Ah, here they both come now."

John turned to see the two men fighting their way against the tide of those who were making their unusually hasty exit. Jerry's expression was unreadable but Catherine's charity manager was looking into John's face and smiling broadly. There was something vaguely familiar about the man.

"Hello Rev," the man said holding out his hand.

"Derek?"

"Yes; sorry I've not seen you for a while, but I've been a bit busy."

John's mouth opened and closed. The change in Derek's appearance was staggering. With such a severe haircut and a smooth, cleanly shaved chin, he looked ten years younger. And his smile! His teeth were now so white, it was impossible to believe that they'd once been so stained.

"I guess you're surprised to see me."

"Yes!" John cried, grasping his hand and pumping it furiously. "And overjoyed. And Jerry, it's great to see you here too."

Jerry shrugged. "I sort of got corralled into coming. Derek can be surprisingly persuasive nowadays."

John looked into Derek's face again. There was indeed a new confidence, a new strength; but there was still that steady calm in his eyes. And it was a peace and humility that put John to shame. "I can imagine," he said with a smile. "Derek, you look amazing – so different that I didn't recognise you."

"I know; I suppose it is a bit of a transformation."

"But how? What happened? I know it's been a month since I last saw you, but even so."

"You can blame Cath; she pretty much dragged me kicking and screaming back into society. It turns out there's a lot more to her than it appears."

"But charity manager? What sort of charity?"

"That's enough!" Catherine chided sharply. "Chit-chat later, business first. I take it you have somewhere other than before the altar for such discussions."

"Yes of course; I'm sorry but I'm just so overwhelmed by everything. I'll finish up here right away."

"Well come along then, chop-chop," Catherine snapped brusquely. "Tempus fugit, and all that."

John looked around. The church was getting very empty now. Never had he seen such indecent haste in vacating the house of God. There seemed little point in waiting at the door and giving the people his usual parting blessing.

"All right then, just give me a moment. I'll tell Graeme that we're shutting up shop early and then I'll slip out of my vestments. After that we can go to the rectory. I'll get Anne to lock up if need be. Can I ask you to wait here?"

"If we must," Catherine replied testily. "But be quick, man; be quick!"

John gave a sharp nod and then hurried over to Anne. His huge grin was so wide it would surely split his cheeks.

CHAPTER TWENTY-TWO –

"I KNOW THAT I WILL LIVE TO SEE THE LORD'S GOODNESS IN THIS PRESENT LIFE. (PSALM 27:13)

A Beginning and an End

John sat back in his armchair and shook his head in disbelief. "This is unbelievable," he murmured incredulously. "I would never have guessed; not in a million years."

"I think that's sort of the point," Derek replied quietly. "Matthew chapter six, verse three, yes?"

John stared at him. Was this really the same man? "Yes, six verse three. *'But when you give alms, do not let your left hand know what your right hand is doing.'*"

The four of them were in the same sitting room in which the bishop had delivered his devastating bombshell; but now a wonderful phoenix was arising from the ashes it had left. John was in the same armchair while Derek was sitting in the one the Right Reverend Anderson had occupied. Catherine was standing behind Derek's chair like a tigress watching over her precious cub. She was being uncharacteristically quiet, giving her protégé free reign in the discussion. Jerry meanwhile was leaning against the wall near the door. He seemed somewhat bored by the whole affair.

"Cath has been quietly doing a lot for people here and there," continued Derek. "But when Sticks died, she felt the need to make things more official. That night I told her all about my past, of what I used to do; so, after the funeral, she asked me – in that irresistible way of hers – to manage the process. The only thing is, we weren't quite sure of what we wanted to do. When we heard about the kitchen though, we discussed it and decided to act at once."

John couldn't help noticing that Derek kept saying, *'we'* and not *'she'*. And nor did Catherine correct him.

"I hope you don't mind me asking, but are you two, you know..."

Both of them looked horrified. "No, we are NOT!" Catherine declared firmly.

"No, no," said Derek at the same time. Then he continued in a more even tone. "Catherine has converted one of her largest bedrooms into a kind of studio flat – more a bedsit really. She's rented it to me and I have the use of one of the bathrooms as well. All in all, it's perfect."

"We share *one* meal a day," Catherine continued coldly. "Breakfast. Eight o'clock sharp. We use that time to discuss the day's business."

"And that business is now to be the kitchen," added Derek with a smile.

"Honestly, this is incredible," John said, once again shaking his head in disbelief. He looked up at Catherine. She was watching him with that disdainful expression that was always so off-putting. "I really don't know how to thank you."

"You can start by asking a fair price for everything," she snapped. "And it's not my doing, it is God's."

Derek leaned earnestly forward. "John, God has been guiding me – *all* of us – toward this for some time now. He began by leading me to the crossroads where I had to confirm or deny my prayer – my cry for help on the steps of my old office. I confirmed it at Kings Cross when I gave myself to Jesus and asked him into my life."

"But today was your first day in church."

"Not quite," replied Derek with an ironic grin. "I've been going to the Baptist Church in Clawdale for a while now. I can understand why some people like the Anglican pomp and ceremony..."

"I like the bells and smells," Catherine interjected with a rare smile.

"...but it doesn't make me feel closer to God. The Baptist Church does, and I didn't feel judged by the people there; no offence intended."

"None taken. But how do you get there?" John asked with a puzzled frown. "It must be a good ten miles away."

"Seven. I didn't actually start going until after Sticks died. Then Catherine dropped me off there every Sunday on her way to your church. It only took her an extra twenty minutes or so. Then, thanks to Cath's insistent encouragement, I managed to get my driving licence back. So the last time I went, I was able to drive myself." He blushed heavily. "Somehow the charity has supplied me with a car."

"I see. But apart from taking on my kitchen, has the charity any other plans?"

Derek sat back in his chair and grinned mischievously. "Oh yes. With god's blessing, the Dean James Memorial Foundation will have soup kitchens in many towns and cities. I'm sure your congregation will be delighted that their complaints have benefitted so many."

"I'm sure they will," chuckled John ironically.

Just then the phone rang. "Excuse me," John said, getting up from the chair. He walked over to it, picked up the hand set and looked at the caller ID. It read 'Bishop'. "Well that didn't take long," groaned John.

"The sky begins to fall, I take it," Catherine remarked sardonically.

"I'm afraid so. I think I'll let the answerphone take his call for now."

But as soon as the answerphone kicked in, the bishop hung up. His message was obviously too important to impart via a mere machine. John breathed a sigh of relief but immediately after that, his mobile rang. Ironically, the ring tone was the pealing bells of Westminster Cathedral. John took it from his jacket pocket and looked at the screen. He groaned again and waited for the joyful sound of the bells to stop ringing.

"Sorry about that," he said with a rueful smile. "I think..." The bells rang out again. Bishop Anderson was definitely not going to give up.

Over by the door, Jerry started laughing. "Well Rev, you're either gonna have to answer it, or turn it off."

"I just don't know what to say to him," replied John. With a heavy sigh, he turned off the phone.

Catherine snorted derisively. "I would have thought it prudent to have planned that before launching into your tirade this morning!"

"I know; I just didn't expect it to blow up in my face so soon."

"What do you think he's going to say?" Derek asked anxiously.

John rubbed a hand across his brow. "I'm not sure. Give me a roasting about my message probably. It wasn't exactly, you know, very Anglican. He'll chew my ear off and tell me to apologise to the congregation, I expect."

"And will you apologise?"

John thought for a moment and then shook his head emphatically. "No; how could I? I feel the Spirit moved me to say what I did; so if I were to retract it, it would be the same as rejecting God."

"So, what are your options?"

"I could ask to be moved to another diocese, I suppose."

"Well that doesn't sound too bad," Derek replied with an oddly sympathetic smile.

"Perhaps not; but I'm not sure I want to do that."

"Will they let you stay if you dig your heels in about the apology?"

"Possibly, but possibly not," sighed John.

"So, what other options would you have?"

"I suppose I would have to step down." He let out a sardonic laugh. "Maybe I should resign from the clergy altogether."

"Don't be ridiculous!" Catherine snapped, even more fervently than usual. "You would lose everything – including a home."

John thought back to his experience on the path outside the church – the moment when all this had begun. He shrugged "If it's a matter of conscience, I'm sure the Lord will provide."

"Oh, come on Rev," Jerry said stepping away from the wall. "Surely you're over reacting. You don't even know what he's going to say yet. He might want to congratulate you for shepherding the flock so strictly."

"And pigs might fly!" John retorted.

"Catherine," Derek said thoughtfully, turning in his chair and looking up at her. "Don't you think all those kitchens could do with a... what do you call them, a chaplain?"

"Hmm... Now there's a thought. Yes, someone to visit each site in turn. Maybe there are more people like Sticks and Derek out there who need spiritual guidance and succour."

"And Jerrys," Derek added with a grin.

"You can leave me out of it," scoffed Jerry. "I prayed once when I was at my most desperate, and I got no answer. I'm not even sure there's anyone there now."

"How do you know he didn't answer?" enquired Derek. "The answer isn't always what we *want*, it's what we *need*. And if your prayer is truly from your heart, it won't be ignored."

"And when did you become so holy?" Jerry sneered angrily.

Derek could see he'd touched a raw nerve. "Sorry Jerry, I was only trying to help."

"Well don't! I'm going outside for some air." With that, he spun on his heels and marched indignantly out of the room.

Both Derek and John watched him go with sad eyes, but Catherine seemed not to notice.

"I was thinking the position should come with a modest property – a small flat perhaps. Of course, the remuneration would be a stipend rather than a salary; but Derek would make sure it's more than sufficient for your needs."

John was flummoxed. "No, I mean yes, I mean..."

"Stop blathering, man. Say what you mean."

"I mean I haven't even decided what I'm doing yet. And anyway, I would have to discuss it all with Anne first; and she's not the sort of person to rush into things."

"Absolutely! I would expect nothing less of her. I'll start looking for properties first thing tomorrow. In fact, I think we'll finish here and reconvene at my house in the morning. Nine o'clock sharp. Probably best to bring your wife along with you."

John looked horrified but Derek winked at him. "It's all right; you'll get used to her."

"That's enough of that!" Catherine scolded sharply. "Come along, Derek, I think John will need to speak to the bishop as soon as possible before the poor man's head explodes – although that might expand his intellect somewhat."

"Catherine!" admonished John. "That's hardly fair."

"Truth is truth," she replied firmly. "Come along Derek, we have things to discuss."

Derek got to his feet and gave John a sympathetic smile. "See you tomorrow; best not to be late. God bless with the bishop."

John nodded mutely and watched the strangely matched pair leave. His mind was now a maelstrom of catastrophe and possibility.

TWENTY-THREE –

"WHOEVER SOWS INJUSTICE REAPS CALAMITY, AND THE ROD THEY WIELD IN FURY WILL BE BROKEN." (PROVERBS 22:8)

Crossroads

Jerry stood at the rectory's front door and watched Derek walk through the gate to where Catherine was waiting for them both in the Land Rover. He couldn't understand what had just happened. When he'd walked out for some air, he'd been angry and defensive, although he had no clue as to why. Yes, he was a fugitive from the law – probably a murderer –

but why would the talk of God and prayer touch a nerve so readily? Guilt perhaps?

He looked at the phone in his hand – Derek's phone. Obviously, his new job came with a lot more than a company car. And there was another puzzle. Why had Derek handed it to him, and why had the reformed drunken dosser felt the need to pray over him? But even more of a mystery, why had he *allowed* Derek to pray over him?

He'd been leaning against the wall, clenching and unclenching both his jaw and his fists when the front door had opened and Catherine and Derek had emerged. He'd been just about to follow them to the car when Derek had stopped him.

"We'll be with you in a moment," he'd called to Catherine. Surprisingly, the abrupt and impatient woman hadn't even turned around. She'd just waved her hand in vague acknowledgement.

"What?" Jerry had asked tersely.

Derek had just given him a strange half smile and had put a consoling hand on the ex-soldier's shoulder.

"I don't know how to put this," Derek had said quietly. "Please don't laugh or get angry; but I've told you what happened at Kings Cross, haven't I?"

"Sort of. You said you sold yourself to Jesus, or something."

"Actually, he'd already bought me. I just needed to acknowledge the fact and give myself to him. But did I ever tell you why I did it at that particular moment?"

Jerry had been oddly intrigued. He'd shaken his head blankly.

"A girl I'd never seen before just walked up to me and gave me her lunchbox. She said she didn't know why; she'd just felt moved to do it by God. Although she knew nothing about me or my troubles, somehow she knew exactly what I needed."

"Her lunch," Jerry had sneered sarcastically.

"Partly; but I needed Christ more than that. As I say, please don't laugh, and please don't be angry, but in the same way, I feel moved to give you this." He had then placed his phone into Jerry's hand. "I feel that God has a plan for you, but there's someone you need to call before he can use you. It's unlocked; just swipe the screen. I'll wait for you in the car and you can give it back in a minute."

"Don't be bloody stupid! Why would God want me to use your phone? And why would he want to use the likes of me anyway?"

"Why would he want to use the likes of me?" Derek had retorted. "But from the moment I said that prayer in Woolwich – the most desperate prayer anyone could ask – he began using me."

"Well *I've* never said a prayer like that!" In spite of his protestation, his despairing plea to the Almighty in the lane near Frinton Wood had come into his head. Angrily he'd pushed the thought away.

"Whatever you say," Derek had said with a shrug. "Still, I'm going to leave the phone with you. Stay here for a few minutes, maybe something will spring to mind. Please Jerry, will you at least do that for me?"

The pleading in Derek's calm, confident eyes had been impossible to deny. "Go on then, only because it's you, though."

"Cheers, pal. One more thing, I have a very strong urge to pray with you. Please, out of friendship, will you let me?"

And so, he had let Derek pray.

"Dear Lord; I have no idea why I'm standing here with my friend, but I know that you do. Please Lord, let Jerry know; let Jerry realise why he needs my phone at this moment. Lord Jesus, I'm sure you have a plan for him; please bless him just like you blessed me. In Jesus name we pray; Amen."

"Amen," Jerry had repeated automatically. Then Derek had squeezed his shoulder and had walked away. But he'd only gone a few steps before he'd turned around.

"One more thing, Jerry; God always give you choices. He gave me the opportunity to come to Rewford, but it was up to me whether I came or not. He put Cath's husband's wallet along with all that money into my hand; but I had the choice as to what I did with it. The right direction is usually signposted, but there's always the temptation to go another way, or just to ignore him altogether." After that rather cryptic statement, the one-time beggar had stridden away.

"So what use is a phone to me anyway?" he mumbled. "Why on Earth would a wanted murderer make such a stupid mistake...?" And then he knew why. Until he knew for sure what the police actually wanted him for – if he was even wanted at all – he couldn't move on with his life. But phone who? The police? That would be a stupid idea – unless it was God's plan for him to go to prison. Was that it? Was he supposed to preach to all the other criminals banged up inside?

Well he can keep that idea to himself, he thought cynically. He'd loved Leanne, and it had been such a tragic accident – one more demon to add to his nightly dose of terror-inducing dreams. Leanne. When she wasn't hormonal, you'd be hard pressed to find a more perfect wife.

Suddenly, he was dialling his old home telephone number. It was so obvious, he couldn't believe why he hadn't thought of it before. If she answered, he was in the clear – at least as far as murder went. And there would hardly be a countrywide manhunt for someone who'd committed a bit of ABH. He would be free to join Derek and Catherine in their soup kitchen venture along with the Rev. Maybe he could give himself to Jesus like Derek had.

Swallowing hard, he lifted the phone to his ear. It rang several times before it was answered.

"Hello?"

His stomach lurched and his heart did a somersault. It was Leanne's voice. All he had to do was hang up and his nightmare was over. God had answered his prayer after all.

But he hesitated. It was *Leanne's* voice. His precious, loving – if occasionally psychotic – wife. The seconds passed. He said nothing, he just listened.

"Hello?" Then came a cynical, "Look, if this is a joke, it's not a clever one. Why don't you go and play with the cars on the motorway."

Still he said nothing and there was no way on Earth that he would. His new free life with his Christian friends would be too wonderful to surrender on a whim. He just wanted to listen to her voice a bit longer. And anyway, she would hang up any moment now.

"Jerry?" she whispered. "Jerry, is that you?" His heart reeled and he almost fell to his knees. And then she was crying softly, weeping bitter tears of regret. "Oh Jerry, I'm so sorry. It was all my own fault, I'm sorry, I'm sorry. Oh, my darling, I promise it'll never happen again. Honestly, I've changed. Please Jerry."

As heartrending as it was, as much as he wanted to answer her and offer some words of comfort, he'd heard it all before. How many women had fallen for the same line over and over again? How many of them – and he had been just as stupid – had believed until it was too late? But he had broken free; it was almost too late, but that life was behind him now. He could now quietly divorce her.

Mind you, didn't he remember the army chaplain reading something from the Bible about divorce? Didn't Jesus say that adultery was the only reason it was allowed. Mentally, he shook his head. No, this was different. Jesus would surely understand these circumstances. But then again, how could his committing such a violent act on a woman be part of a loving God's plan?

His indecision was unbearable, but then came another voice from the phone. Someone was in the room with her.

"Oi, who you talkin' to? It better not be another bloke or you're for it. Is it that geezer who was eyeing you up in the pub the other night? It better not be!"

So, she had another man in her life already. The pang of jealousy was quickly overwhelmed by a feeling of relief. He *was* free after all.

Thank you Jesus, he thought fervently.

And then he heard, "Gimme that phone! Go on give it to me, bitch!" Leanne yelped with pain, whether from a blow or simply from the handset being wrenched from her hand he couldn't tell.

A wry and bitter smile twisted his lips. After all the abuse and violence she'd bestowed on him, she was now getting a taste of her own medicine. Again, he went to hang up but this time the man spoke.

"Who the hell are you?" he demanded. "Come on, say something."

It would have been funny if it hadn't been so tragic. Poor Leanne. What a sad and disastrous turn of events. He sighed heavily; perhaps he could get Derek to pray for her. With a burst of joy, he realised there was nothing to stop him praying for her himself. Perhaps one day, when his new life had been established, the Lord would bring the two of them back together in a more peaceful, harmonious relationship.

Thank you Jesus!

"If you're that bloke from the pub, I'm gonna break your legs, and I'll break hers an' all! Now who the hell are you?"

An inferno of indignation welled up inside Jerry as surely as magma rose up inside a volcano. But when it erupted an instant later, there was no hot and concussive explosion; there was just a tight, sub-zero certainty; a fury as cold and as still as death itself. All thoughts of his new Christian life in Rewford were now entombed in impenetrable ice. He could always forgive Leanne, but this man had just booked himself a date with destruction, and a bed in intensive care.

"I'm her husband," he said in a voice frosted with cold menace. "And I'll be home tomorrow…"

.

Printed in Great Britain
by Amazon

74508217R00139